Way Down Dead in Dixie

Also by Caroline Cousins

Fiddle Dee Death

Marsh Madness

Way Down Dead in Dixie

Caroline Cousins

JOHN F. BLAIR
PUBLISHER
Winston-Salem, North Carolina

Published by John F. Blair, Publisher

*The paper in this book meets the guidelines
for permanence and durability of the Committee on Production
Guidelines for Book Longevity of the Council on Library Resources.*

Cover photo by Thomas P. Warner

Library of Congress Cataloging-in-Publication Data

Cousins, Caroline.
    Way down dead in Dixie / by Caroline Cousins.
        p.   cm.
    ISBN-13: 978-0-89587-335-4 (hardcover : alk. paper)
    ISBN-10: 0-89587-335-4 (hardcover : alk. paper)
    ISBN-13: 978-0-89587-336-1 (pbk. : alk. paper)
    ISBN-10: 0-89587-336-2 (pbk.: alk. paper)
1. Women detectives—South Carolina—Fiction. 2. Real estate developers—
Fiction. 3. Plantation life—Fiction. 4. South Carolina—Fiction. 5. Cousins—
Fiction. I. Title.
PS3603.0888W39 2007
813'.6—dc22
                        2007006632

For the family, always

And in memory of:

Phoebe Jane Herndon, May 24, 1926–February 14, 2005

Donald Rosmond Pate, November 7, 1923–December 8, 2005

James Francis Greer, May 24, 1929–April 14, 2006

Prologue

On the hottest night of the year, the three met in the graveyard for the last time. The full moon elongated the shadows of the tall trees and leaning headstones. The air was as heavy and still as the Spanish moss draping the sloping limbs of the live oak tree near the back fence.

This was their favorite place, next to the Colonel's marble tomb. No one saw them as they discussed the plans for their trip, smoked and laughed, shared a bottle of wine and secrets.

Or so they thought.

Hidden in the thick underbrush, he watched and listened, a feral smile twisting his lips. This wasn't the first time he had crouched here. They didn't know he spied on them or how he felt, the mix of curiosity and envy, the anger even he didn't understand. They didn't know. He dug his fingers in the dirt. He watched. He waited.

CHAPTER ONE

Hasn't She Died Before?

At exactly six o'clock in the evening on the last Sunday in June, the double mahogany doors opened wide.

"Welcome to Pinckney Plantation."

I said the words automatically, even though I recognized most of the well-dressed men and women assembled on the wide front porch. Not the usual lineup of sandal-shod, T-shirted tourists, their sunburned faces agog at finally being allowed access to the inner sanctum, these were all islanders who took the faded antebellum grandeur for granted. Pinckney Plantation and Indigo Island have been inseparable for going on two centuries.

"Miss Eliza is in the back parlor," said my cousin Bonnie in hushed tones, gesturing toward the hallway leading past the sweeping staircase.

The Hendersons, who lived down at the beach near my parents, edged into the shadowed room, followed by others who nodded politely as they filed past.

"Lindsey, Bonnie, thank you." Ray Simmons ushered in his wife, Sally, who was trying her best to contain her bubbly personality.

"It is so good of Miss Augusta to have us all here," she said. "I know Miss Eliza's house is in no shape for company. I'm sure Fort appreciates it. How's he doing?"

I didn't dare look at Bonnie. "About as well as can be expected."

Ray raised one dark eyebrow. "That well?" He tipped an imaginary flask to his lips.

"Stop, sugar," Sally admonished. "This has got to be hard on him, bless his heart. Such a shock."

"Hardly," Ray said. Maybe being a hotshot developer made him cynical. Then again, Fort Bailey's taste for bourbon and branch was well known, much to his teetotaling mother's chagrin. "Miss Eliza's been threatening to go anytime the last five years."

"I know, I know." Sally put her hand on his arm to lead him toward the hallway. "When I heard about it yesterday and called my sister in Charleston, she said she thought Miss Eliza had died before. Now, I know she didn't leave Comfort's End much, but I think Sister was confusing her with this other Mrs. Bailey. She wasn't a Comfort, though, like Eliza. I'm not even sure I know her people. I'll have to ask Cora. She's here, of course."

Bonnie smiled politely. "With Miss Maudie and Miss Augusta."

Cora, our great-aunt, is best friends with the other two widows. They were all girls together on the island eighty-plus years ago, as was Eliza Comfort Bailey. Eliza was a tad older but still a member of their bridge club until her health began going downhill. Even then, she invited the other ladies to bring their pineapple-and-cream-cheese sandwiches over to the big house at Comfort's End for Monday lunch and bridge. "I know it's not Pinckney," she told them, acknowledging her and her home's decline as she expertly dealt the cards with arthritic fingers. "But I have to save my energy for playing. Two diamonds."

Miss Eliza always opened with diamonds even if she didn't have any. Happily, her friends were used to "Eliza's little ways," as they referred to her list of eccentricities. Which was why people were paying their respects to her in the back parlor at Pinckney instead of the funeral parlor in Centerville, the county seat, over the drawbridge and twenty miles inland.

"I still think it's sort of creepy," Bonnie said, shutting the heavy door against the wall of hot air.

"I know what you mean," I agreed. "But Miss Eliza's last request was to be 'laid out and candle-lit.' She made Miss Augusta promise to have it here. You know, they used to do it all the time, have the visitation at home. Those really old houses with the narrow winding stairs have niches in the wall so they could bring down a coffin."

"I thought it was so they could bring the beds up."

"Whatever." I wiped some beads of sweat off my brow. "Lordy, it's hot. Let's just be happy for A.C."

Before Miss Augusta opened her family's ancestral home to the public, she decided to put in central heat and air. It was an expense that had paid off, not only in the hordes of tourists seeking refuge from the sultry summers of the South Carolina Low Country but also because she was able to hire help. Bonnie and I, along with Bonnie's older sister, Margaret Ann, had been among the first tour guides when we were in high school. The costumes were lightweight knockoffs of Scarlett O'Hara attire, but we still would have keeled over from heatstroke if we had on our belle-wear without air conditioning.

"I expect they had some quick funerals back then." Bonnie wrinkled her perfect nose. "Was Miss Eliza related to the Pinckneys, too?"

"Somehow," I replied, trying to visualize the intertwining branches of the island families' trees. "But it may have been by marriage instead of blood. Like us. Or it could be by both. Like us."

Our family ties are tightly knotted. Our mothers are sisters and our fathers are first cousins, which makes us "one-and-a-half-times first cousins," as Margaret Ann likes to say, adding quickly that "it's all legal 'cause our mothers didn't marry their first cousins."

That's true, except that way back in the late 1700s, Indigo and its big sister, Edisto Island, were settled by a handful of British colonists, our ancestors among them. Over the years, they'd intermarried enough that the same surnames kept turning up in successive generations.

"Who's like us?" Margaret Ann piped up from the hallway in one of her stage whispers that can be heard a country mile. Her hearing is just as acute, especially if she thinks she's being left out of an interesting conversation. Or any conversation.

"We were trying to figure out if Miss Eliza is somehow kin to the Pinckneys," Bonnie replied in a normal voice, now that her sister had joined us by the door.

"Probably," Margaret Ann said blithely. "Miss Eliza had those pale blue eyes, although that might have been cataracts. And besides, you can't always go by looks. Look at us." She waved her hand at me. "I've got blue eyes, but yours and Bonnie's are green, and Bonnie's been a blonde since she was a baby, even if she needs some help now. But your hair's practically black, and I'm in between, just like in age."

Good grief. She never forgets that she's all of two days younger than I am.

"I'm the tallest." Bonnie stated the obvious. "And the thinnest." She smirked.

"Not so much anymore. After thirty-five, your metabolism slows down. I keep telling you, you better watch how many biscuits you eat for breakfast."

"Yes, Mam," Bonnie said, winking at me. Margaret Ann's nickname is "Mam" because of her initials. She was a Mikell before she married J. T., who was conveniently named Matthews.

"Y'all come on in the back parlor now," Mam said. "Miss Augusta's expecting us. And then you can show people out through the dining room like on tour. That way, they can stick to the runners. Sally's got on spike heels for some reason, and we don't want her on the heart pine."

I agreed. Mam might sound like the mistress of the plantation—and she does run the gift shop, along with her own specialty floral business—but I've been the manager the last few months since

I moved back to Indigo. If anything happened to the floors or furnishings, I'd be the one who had to answer to Miss Augusta Pinckney Townsend, or worse, her equally elderly housekeeper, Marietta Manigault. It was Marietta who had insisted we stop the grandfather clock and drape the downstairs mirrors for this evening. "Matter of respect," she'd sniffed, handing me a length of black crepe. "We do things proper at Pinckney, even if some folk don't give a lick."

I knew she meant Miss Eliza's sole survivor, Comfort Bailey, a.k.a. "Fort," who was standing near the parlor fireplace looking like a man in need of a drink. Tall, with receding faded blond hair, he was your typical high-school football player gone to seed in his sixties. Still, his dissipated good looks and hearty manner stood out in a crowd. He was talking to Otis Heywood, the short, rotund funeral director, but his eyes were on Sally's shapely legs in her too-high heels.

Otis, meanwhile, was looking with satisfaction at Miss Eliza, who was indeed "laid out and candle-lit" on a bier that I knew was made with a couple of sawhorses and some plywood. But Mam had covered it like a cake table at one of her wedding receptions, swagging yards of the material Miss Augusta had bought in bulk from Wal-Mart for the tour-guide costumes.

"Pinckney purple," Bonnie whispered in my ear. "I should have known."

"From here to eternity." I was trying to avoid the coffin, unlike Mam, who had marched right over for a little look-see.

"Otis did a good job," she pronounced on her return. "That assistant of his didn't get carried away with the Maybelline, like he's been known to do. Hey, Sally," she said, turning her head, "cute shoes."

"Oh, thank you," Sally said. "They're about to kill me. Oops." She put her hand to her mouth. "That's not the best choice of words in the circumstances." She looked around to see if anyone had heard, then leaned in closer. "I came to tell you Fort is planning the estate sale for Thursday."

We all snapped to attention.

"Well, he's not wasting any time." Mam was practically twitching with excitement.

"He's been ready ever since Miss Eliza had that bad spell at Easter. Y'know, he's already had everything appraised by some expert in Charleston." Sally, who had a small antiques shop, sounded miffed. "I think he probably called in the ad to the papers along with his mama's obituary. Wants a head start on the crowds for the Fourth. It doesn't seem quite proper, but Ray says he needs the money, got in over his head on some land deal in Florida that got put back 'cause of the hurricanes."

"Is having the sale so quick legal, Bonnie?" Mam asked.

"I guess so," Bonnie said. "I'm not that kind of lawyer. I do know that Fort can't sell Comfort's End except to the state. It's in the eminent-domain zone for whenever they build a new bridge."

"Yes." Sally nodded. "Ray says developers aren't going anywhere near the north peninsula until the surveys are done and the tree huggers stop complaining."

Bonnie started to say something—being an environmental lawyer, she's often an advocate for wildlife groups and preservation trusts—but Mam jumped in. "What all's in the sale, Sally? I haven't been in Comfort's End in years."

"Everything, I hear. Furniture, jewelry, silver, china, housewares—the whole ball of wax. Between the Baileys and the Comforts, Miss Eliza was well fixed, even if Fort has let the house go. His ex-wives all took cash, although I think one of them did get to keep the Bailey pearls."

"I've got pearls," Mam said. "I need more stuff for my new sunroom."

"I'm hunting a partner's desk for Tom," Bonnie said, referring to her husband, a lieutenant commander in the navy. "I'd like to get it while he's on cruise this summer and have it when he comes home in the fall."

Sally considered. "I think there was one in the study. Or maybe it was upstairs. Oak, good condition."

"Ooh, a partner's desk!" Mam chimed in. "J. T. would like that, too."

"First dibs, sister dear."

"Don't be too sure about that." Mam's voice was rising. "How would you get a desk back to D.C. anyhow? Your minivan was stuffed with you and the boys coming down."

"I'll figure something out." Bonnie wasn't about to let Mam horn in on her coveted treasure. "And J. T. has a desk. You don't need—"

"—to be so loud," I cut in. "Miss Augusta's giving us the look."

The piercing blue eyes over the beaky nose had turned our way.

"Uh-oh," Bonnie said. "Remember where you are, girls."

"I'll go speak to her and Miss Maudie," Sally said. "Then Ray and I need to go."

The room was already clearing out. Aunt Cora, short and spry, was by the far door, gently herding the Hendersons on their way. Ray was talking to Fort and Otis. Miss Maudie was fiddling with her hearing aid as Sally chattered. And Marietta, who had slipped in quietly, stood next to the heavy drapes shielding the room from the early-evening glare. She was staring at Miss Eliza with a strange expression on her face. Even as I directed Mam's and Bonnie's eyes toward her, Marietta moved close to the gleaming wooden box. One hand resting on a brass handle, she put the other on the white tufted satin ruche that ran around the rim like cake frosting. Her fingers were tightly clenched. What was she holding?

Mam drew a quick breath, but Bonnie poked her before she could say anything. "Shh."

I could see Marietta's lips moving. Was she praying? Her eyes were closed. Then her right hand disappeared into the depths of the coffin.

Chapter Two
For Better or Curse

"What do you think is in the coffin?" Bonnie asked.

"Besides Miss Eliza?"

"Shh, Lindsey," Mam half-giggled, "or we'll have Aunt Cora over here again."

No sooner had the three of us spied Marietta's odd behavior than our aunt interrupted, wanting to know if we'd heard from our parents yet today.

"Mama called this afternoon," Mam said. "They really like this Alaska cruise, especially the change in the weather. They bought sweatshirts in the ship's store. Of course, they were sorry to hear about Miss Eliza."

Sorry they were missing this, I thought. Given the choice between an island funeral and a midnight buffet, they might forgo the baked Alaska, seeing as how they were eating every three hours, to hear our mamas tell it. It was just as well Miss Eliza's interment was a simple affair, with the visitation this evening and a graveside service in the morning, no hors d'oeuvres involved.

Aunt Cora tsked at our parents' globetrotting since our daddies' retirements last year. She often visited relatives, but never above the Mason-Dixon line or west of the Mississippi. By the time she moved on to Miss Maudie, who was nodding off in her chair next to a thriving aspidistra, Marietta had left the room.

Mam contemplated the coffin. "We could go see." She sounded doubtful.

"You can, but I bet Marietta hid whatever it is." No way was I going to disturb the eternally resting Miss Eliza. "It might be some Gullah charm."

"Marietta doesn't practice voodoo!" Mam was aghast. "She goes to Mount Zion A.M.E. and sings in the choir."

"I didn't say anything about voodoo. But you know Marietta is superstitious. She's the one who stopped the clocks. And Miss Augusta may not talk about Pinckney's ghost, but Marietta doesn't go up in the attic."

Bonnie was momentarily diverted. "Anything new from the ghost, Lindsey?"

"No, except Miss Augusta finally let me put something in the guides' script that the attic is said to be haunted by a young woman disappointed in love."

"There's more to the legend than that!" Bonnie began building her case. "Having your father shoot your Yankee soldier lover and then bleeding to death because you put your arm through a window trying to warn him is not exactly 'disappointed in love.' And what about the crazy Pinckney locked in the cage?"

"Oh, come on," I said. "Miss Augusta's never going to acknowledge that story. I only convinced her to get in what I did by telling her it was good for tourists and that we were the only plantation without a ghost in residence."

"And now we have a coffin in the parlor," Bonnie said. "How's that for a tourist attraction?"

"It won't be here after tonight." Mam headed for the kitchen. "And I want to know what's in it now. Besides Miss Eliza."

❦

"Marietta, Lindsey says you put some sort of Gullah curse in with Miss Eliza."

"That is not what I said!" I couldn't believe Mam, twisting my words like that. "I said maybe it was a charm or something."

Marietta looked up from stirring a glass of iced tea. "Or something. Hmm." She carefully set the spoon on a white napkin on the scarred oak table. "Some folks say that family already cursed."

"How so?" Bonnie asked.

"Since when?" I wanted to know how many generations of Comforts and Baileys we were dealing with.

"Was it a voodoo hex?" Mam had voodoo on the brain.

Marietta motioned for us to pour our own tea from the glass pitcher sitting on the counter and pushed a saucer toward me. "Here's the lemon and the mint." She waited until we were all seated. "It was some years after the war."

We knew she meant the Civil War. That's the only war on Indigo. Yankee troops occupied the island then, the officers quartering at Pinckney. Most of the white islanders fled upstate, although Rebel militia at Adams Run made forays through the countryside between Charleston and Beaufort.

"They didn't call it Comfort's End then," Marietta continued. "It was Comfort's Crossing 'cause there was a landing where the steamboats stopped before they got to Edisto."

"And Bailey's ferry went from there across to the mainland at the Dawhoo Cut," I supplied. "I wrote about it in my history column for the paper this week, about how there was the ferry and then the causeway and then a makeshift bridge."

"What does that have to do with a curse?" Mam asked. She is so impatient.

"I don't know," I said. "I thought it was Comfort's End because it was at the end of that part of the island. Y'know, like Land's End."

Marietta nodded. "That was later, after the big storm."

Again, we knew she was talking about the hurricane of 1893, which had wreaked destruction across Indigo, felling trees, shifting sands, and drowning unlucky islanders in the storm surge.

"The wind washed off that part of the island, and it took a

graveyard with it," Marietta said. "All the coffins and the markers went out to sea, and nobody not ever see those bones again."

"Golly," Bonnie said. "So that's why Miss Eliza's being buried at Indigo Hill. I wondered how come they didn't have a family cemetery like the Pinckneys."

"Folks started calling it Comfort's End after that, saying the land was cursed and so were the Comforts, because so many of them come to a bad end. Course, lots of people die young back then—babies get the fever, men in wars and such—but it did seem like the Comforts make a habit of it. Miss Eliza's daddy was snakebit, and her mother died birthing her brother. Then he fell off a horse and broke his neck. Her husband, he have a bad heart and leave her with the two boys."

"Fort has a brother?" Mam, who prides herself on island genealogy, was surprised.

"Had." Marietta pursed her lips. "Frank Jr. went in the army, and he killed over in Korea. Later, his wife—she from Mississippi—she die in a automobile accident. That when Becky come live on Indigo."

"Becky?" The name was new to all of us.

"Miss Eliza's granddaughter, Becky Bailey. She only here a few years. Went off right after high school to see her mama's people and done drown in Hurricane Camille."

"Wow!" Bonnie's tea went down the wrong way, and she started coughing. Mam leaned over to whack her baby sister in the back, but Bonnie saw her coming and stood up, warding her off. She'd experienced too many of Mam's well-meaning thumps over the years. "I'm okay," she snuffled. "Just give me a sec." She drew a deep breath. "I never knew any of this."

Neither did I, but my ex-reporter's nose smelled a good story. I wondered if I could use any of this in my next history column for the *Centerville Times*. I'd have to ask the weekly's editor, Ravenel Wade Hampton III. R. W. might even have known Becky Bailey, if his tales of his glory days covering student protests and Jane Fonda at UNC-Chapel Hill, my alma mater, were anything to go by. He'd be about the right age.

"When was Camille?" Mam was staring at the building-supply calendar tacked on the pantry door as if it had the answer.

"Summer 1969," I said. "Same as Woodstock and right after Neil Armstrong walked on the moon. Our daddies took us outside on the beach and said there really was a man on the moon."

"You remember that? We were awful little."

"Not really. At least I don't think so, but I've heard Daddy talk about it so much I feel like I do."

"They were always taking us out on the beach in our baby-doll pajamas after supper." Mam sounded so wistful I could almost smell the Noxzema on our sunburns. "Then we'd come back and sit on the screen porch, and the grownups would talk and tell stories." She looked accusingly at Marietta. "But I don't remember anything about the Comforts and a curse."

"Could be they didn't know, or they heard it and didn't believe it." Marietta stood up. "Spell's not much good if you not believe in it. That what my granny used to say."

"Miss Eliza must not have because she sure didn't die young." Bonnie paused from gathering up our glasses. "Maybe that was her curse, outliving all her family but Fort. Poor Miss Eliza."

Marietta didn't say anything. I put a piece of tinfoil over the lemon and stuck it in the refrigerator next to the family-sized jar of Duke's mayonnaise.

"Well, was that it, Marietta?" Mam handed me the tea pitcher to shove in between the orange juice and the Coke. "Did you give Miss Eliza a charm?"

Still no answer. Hunched over the kitchen sink with her back to us, her graying, dark hair tightly drawn in a bun, Marietta looked like someone in a storybook, a wise old woman who knew her way around a spell or two. That is, if you didn't look at her feet in white Nikes right out of Wimbledon. And the Pinckney purple socks.

"Marietta?" Mam wheedled. "What did you put in with Miss Eliza?"

Bonnie and I looked at each other. It was a tossup as to who was the more stubborn. Mam could be as pesky as a mosquito, but

Marietta was like a clam when she got in a mood.

"Marietta?" There was that mosquito whine.

"Leave off, Mam," Bonnie said. "It's not your secret. If Marietta doesn't want to tell us, she doesn't have to."

Marietta turned and looked sternly at Mam. "If I tells you, you best not be telling Miss Augusta. I should never have told you 'bout the curse in the first place. I just make up a little potion like my granny used to. And no, I not telling you what all in it."

Mam's eyes widened. "It doesn't have blood in it, does it? If there's blood, Lindsey will get sick." She looked at me expectantly.

I'd just as soon not know what was in any secret potion, especially if there was blood or innards. I'd never have made it through biology in high school if Mam hadn't been my lab partner and sawed on that smelly frog. I felt my stomach twitch.

Bonnie saved me. "We don't care what's in it, just what it's for."

Marietta leaned back and folded her arms. "It to help Miss Eliza change her ways so she can get in heaven."

"What ways?" Mam the mosquito. "Why would Miss Eliza need help? She was a Presbyterian."

"I know," I said, remembering something I'd heard. "It's because of Mauma Christine, isn't it? Miss Eliza didn't want her as a nurse, even though she was the best on the island."

Marietta nodded. "She wouldn't have black help. Comforts never have, not since they come back after the war."

"Isn't that illegal?" Mam looked perplexed.

"Not if it's your house," Bonnie said. "It's just racist."

"Only they don't see it that way," I pointed out. "Think of that trashy crowd up near Copperhead Creek. I heard Eddie Smoak got himself in with some white-power group up in the pen."

"The Comforts aren't like that," Mam said. "Miss Eliza was D.A.R. and U.D.C., but so are Aunt Cora and Miss Augusta. They're not racists."

"No one said they were," Bonnie said. "And neither is every redneck good ol' boy with a shotgun in the back of his truck or every sorority girl with her Stars and Bars beach towel. Goodness knows, we see enough racial profiling and ethnic stereotyping in D.C. And you taught enough school kids, Mam, to know color doesn't come into consideration when brains are handed out."

"Who's handing out what?" Aunt Cora took us by surprise.

"Oatmeal cookies." Marietta reached for the large red tin. "I made them before church this morning so you ladies could have them with your bridge game."

"Bridge game?" Mam jumped in first, even as Bonnie moved toward the cookies. "Who's playing bridge?"

"We are," Aunt Cora said. "I came in to see if you'd help me set up the card table and chairs in the parlor."

"Now?" I was confused.

"Of course now." Aunt Cora was her usual brisk self. "What, didn't Augusta tell you we're sitting up with Eliza tonight?"

"No, ma'am, she didn't." I looked at my cousins, who shook their heads. None of us had planned on staying awake for a wake.

"How are you going to play bridge?" Mam asked. "You aren't counting on us, are you? I told J. T. I'd be home about now, and Bonnie has to pick up the boys and get them to bed. I guess Lindsey could be your fourth. She doesn't have anything to do since Will's away, although Bonnie will have to go let Doc out and feed Peaches, or maybe Lindsey could go and come back—"

Aunt Cora tried to interrupt the cascade of words. "Margaret Ann! We don't need a fourth. We'll play three-handed."

"Does that mean . . . ?" Bonnie's voice trailed off, an oatmeal cookie halfway to her mouth.

"Yes, Eliza will be the dummy. It might seem strange to some, but we've done it before on her bad days. She didn't mind a bit."

She certainly wasn't in a position to mind now.

"But how do you decide who's going to be her partner?" I was curious. "How can you bid? You don't know what's in her hand."

"It doesn't matter." Aunt Cora smiled. "We let her go first, and she always opens with a diamond."

February 9

Grandmother was high score at bridge today, so she was in a good mood at supper. I decided to ask her if I could wear her necklace for the Valentine's dance. She made that face she always makes when I ask for anything and said she'd think about it. That's something. If not, I guess I can wear the red velvet band as a choker. She's only letting me go because J. is going. She doesn't need to know about R. She'd ask too many questions. She doesn't like me to have secrets. That's a laugh. She thinks I'm doing my English homework now, but I've already finished it, and my math, too. I hate math. I guess I'll work on history. Remember the Maine! Grandmother's cousin was in the Spanish-American War in Cuba. There's a marker in the graveyard.

Chapter Three

Grave Secrets

Bonnie's diamond glinted in the sun as she pulled on a pair of hot-pink gardening gloves exactly matching her designer overalls.

"Are you the rosy fingers of dawn?" I yawned while lacing up my ancient hiking boots. They were hot and heavy as the morning air but good protection when tromping around in the underbrush. So was the bug spray I handed over to Bonnie. Once we started pulling at weeds and bushes, every bit of exposed skin would be a magnet for mosquitoes. "Don't forget the back of your neck." Both of us had put our hair in ponytails clamped up with barrettes. With our purple Pinckney Plantation baseball caps and oversized sunglasses, we looked like radioactive insects.

"Phew!" Bonnie sneezed. "I feel like I've showered in Pine-Sol."

"Think of the scent as Christmas trees." I wiped my forehead. My bangs were already wet. "And pretend it's winter." I stepped over the clippers and rake she had pitched on the patchy grass and stood beside her. We both sighed.

This was going to be a chore, no matter that Mam called it "a little project." It was probably twentieth on her list today. She was a few miles away on project nineteen, gathering up empty flower containers used in a wedding last weekend. She'd insisted that Bonnie and I go ahead and start whacking away at the vegetation that made Nanny's grave site look like a mysterious ruin in a long-lost jungle. We couldn't have "our people" looking bedraggled with Miss Eliza's funeral being held in a few hours.

Several plots over near a large live oak, the Roe brothers were about halfway finished with her grave, judging from the clumps of black dirt mixed with grassy turf in their battered wheelbarrow. They were doing it the old-fashioned way, with shovels, a pickax, muscle, and sweat. Out here on the island, tractors and backhoes can damage the old graves dug side by side, some family members now close in death even though they hadn't spoken to one another in life. Both the tall tombstones with winged angels reaching heavenward and the age-smoothed markers on forgotten graves hindered heavy equipment. Two rutted gravel paths—just wide enough for a hearse—formed a cross on Indigo Hill. The name is misleading. The cemetery across King's Road from Pinckney may have a slight rise near the middle, but it's still at sea level, like the rest of the island.

Our people—Lindseys, Foxes, Hills, Mikells—lie in the far left quadrant, nudging up against the old metal-and-wire fence half hidden by honeysuckle and wisteria. A couple of tall pines and oaks provide shade, as well as ropelike roots that have cracked several markers over time.

"Who is Albert"—Bonnie tugged at a stubborn leafy vine—"Owen Hill?" She peered at the gray granite.

"Nanny's daddy, our great-grandfather."

"I thought that was Shug."

"One and the same." I clipped away at an especially hearty azalea to reveal another stone, this one heart shaped. "He was the baby of the family, and they just called him Shug for Sugar. Then when he was twelve, he chose his own name. But they still called him Shug. I think this is his sister, Great-Aunt Eunice."

Bonnie wiped the perspiration off her nose, leaving a black smudge. "I know the parents come out here and do flowers and clear out pretty often, but isn't there a caretaker? Ol' what's-his-name, Hip Hop?"

"You mean Rabbit?" I sat back on my knees. "Oh, he just comes by on his own schedule. Rabbit Hare."

"That can't be his real name."

"I think he was christened Robert. Poor guy, he's a couple bricks shy of a load. He keeps an eye on the gate and chases away any kids that come down here at night."

Bonnie raked her mix of twigs, leaves, and vines into a pile, the pine needles sticking up like quills. "The Colonel's tomb still the attraction?"

"So I hear." I looked over to the marble mausoleum the size of a playhouse that housed the remains of one of the island's Civil War veterans and his two wives. Situated near the back fence at the cemetery's center, it was hidden from the road by another grand old oak. For years, bold island teens had used the memorial bench beneath it as a meeting spot to smoke and drink, telling ghost stories so the girls would squeal and have an excuse to hug on the guys. "Rabbit's called the deputies a couple times when he thought there were more of them than he could handle."

"So he's a scaredy Rabbit?" Bonnie grinned as she rested on the rake for a minute.

"Scary is more like it. He looks like some sort of swamp rat. You'll see. I'm surprised he's not here yet, but neither is Otis. He'll have the burial vault for the casket."

"I want to know where Mam is. I don't suppose you can get a cell signal from here."

"Not unless you climb a tree. We're in a dead spot." I tossed my azalea clippings on Bonnie's pile. "Literally."

"Ha-ha." Bonnie went back to raking. "I wish we had a wheelbarrow. If Mam doesn't have one, I'm going to ask the Roes if we can borrow theirs. Is that Randy or Ricky dumping the fill dirt by the fence? I never remember which is which. He looks hot."

"No kidding. Maybe because it is hot. Humid, too."

"No, I mean hot as in *hot*. He took his shirt off."

I saw the tan, muscled back. "That's Ricky," I said. "He's about twenty years younger than Randy. Don't you remember him from high school?"

"He didn't look like that in high school. I would have noticed. Yum!"

"Bonnie Lynn Tyler! How long has your husband been at sea?"

"Too long. There's nothing wrong with looking—which you still are, cousin dear. When did you say Will was coming back?"

"I didn't." Trying to keep private my rediscovered romance with the island's chief deputy was practically futile where family was concerned. Or anyone on the island, for that matter. At least no one knew that Will had been my secret college love before he jilted me for his high-school honey. She'd left him a couple years ago for a state legislator when they were living in Columbia. Will had returned to Indigo last summer, and we had reconnected right after Christmas. He'd been one of the reasons I moved back to the island from Charlotte. Only now, he was temporarily working on some special drug task force somewhere in the Southeast. "Actually, I don't know that he even knows. Sometime soon, I hope." My turn to shock Bonnie. "I am so tired of cold showers."

"Lindsey Lee Fox!" Her outraged yelp was so satisfactory I started laughing. "Stop it, Lindsey, or I'm going to get you with this rake. I can't believe we are having this conversation in a cemetery."

"Good a place as any. Maybe more so. You can't tell me we'd be related to all these people if it weren't for sex."

"True, but I still feel like I want to put my hands over Nanny's marker."

"She outlived three husbands."

"And she went to her grave not knowing you ran off and got married that summer before you were twenty and then got divorced two months later."

"She wouldn't have minded me getting married—she left me her wedding rings—but she wouldn't have looked kindly on me leaving Dennis, even though he was a Yankee."

"You got the wedding rings? I thought our mamas had them."

"Mine. All mine. Also her mother's. And her first engagement ring."

"I knew you had the opal, but your birthday's in September,

not October. Opals are unlucky unless they're your birthstone."

"I don't believe that. Besides, I'm a Libra. It's my astrological stone."

"You've got the platinum with all the little diamonds?" Bonnie seemed a bit put out.

"She thought I wasn't going to get a wedding ring, that I was going to be an old maid." I looked at the vine Bonnie was viciously yanking out of the ground. "Bonnie, be careful! That's poison ivy."

"Yikes! I don't think I got any on me. The leaves are huge, though. I hope it's not that super-poison kind. I'm glad I didn't bring the boys."

"Who's having Vacation Bible School this week?"

"The Baptists. They went to the Methodists last week." She held the ivy vine away from her. "What should I do with this?"

"Here, give it to me. I'll go throw it over the back fence. Hey, there's Mam. See if she has a wheelbarrow."

I picked my way through the graveyard toward the Colonel's tomb. Our plot was getting pretty crowded, but I knew there was room for me next to Mother and Daddy. The cousins had laid claim near Aunt Boodie and Uncle James. Mam told J. T. he could go across the road with the Matthewses, but she wasn't having any part of the "new" cemetery, which was only a century old.

"Tom wants his ashes scattered at sea," Bonnie had said at the time.

"Good," Mam replied. "Otherwise, we might have to bury you standing up."

I smiled at the memory. Some people might think we were morbid, but I found our conversations comforting. And as Bonnie said wryly, we probably won't have to worry about getting into heaven. "We're like our mamas and Nanny. We can talk our way in anywhere."

Mmm. That reminded me of Miss Eliza and what Marietta had said. And what she hadn't said. But I was pretty sure that it did have something to do with the old lady's segregationist views. The island's original wealth—first its indigo dye, then sea-island cotton—had been built on the backs of slaves, and there were reminders everywhere, including this cemetery, of a past both proud and shameful. But for years now, the island had moved with the times, albeit somewhat slowly on occasion. Miss Eliza was among the last of her kind. If Fort shared her presumed prejudices, he was too much the businessman to show them. Although it had been businessmen who once hid behind white sheets . . .

"Lindsey." Mam's voice carried past where the Glovers, the McTeers, and rows of Padgetts were peacefully resting. Or not. Mam's voice is loud enough to wake the dead.

"Over here!" I yelled back, pitching the poison ivy over the fence into the dense woods. I immediately lost sight of it in the lush, snaky undergrowth.

"Guess what!" Mam trotted up, waving her arms in excitement. "The bridge is out. A barge hit it. I heard it from Sally Simmons."

The old hinged drawbridge that cranked open horizontally, swinging to one side, got stuck every now and then. It was the main reason for a new concourse arching high enough above the Intracoastal Waterway to allow for both boats and barges below and cars and trucks atop. The drawbridge wasn't just an inconvenience; safety issues were involved. The bridge was the only way on and off the island except by boat. Helicopters could do emergency medical evacuations, but heaven forbid a hurricane sent everybody fleeing for higher ground at the same time.

"They're postponing the funeral until tomorrow." Mam's words tumbled out even faster than usual. "The minister's here, but Otis and the vault for Miss Eliza are on the other side."

"Where's Miss Eliza?"

"In her coffin. Oh, you mean *where*. Still in the parlor. I was at Pinckney when we heard about the bridge. There's a crew coming from Charleston to fix it, but it's going to take awhile, plus the safety inspectors have to certify everything. Miss Augusta says we'll just keep the parlor closed to visitors today. She's worried we won't get any tourists."

"Not unless they're already on the island." I looked at the sky.

"If it rains this afternoon, bored people will show up at Pinckney because they can come inside."

"They could go to the Gatortorium," Bonnie said. "It's got a reptile house."

Mam shuddered. She's phobic about snakes.

I pulled off my gardening gloves. "Well, what a mess. And Monday's check-in day for all the Monday-to-Monday renters. The phone must be ringing off the hook at the real-estate office."

"And the sheriff's office." Mam looked at me pointedly. "If Will was here, we'd know what was going on."

"You seem to have a pretty good idea. You could call Olivia. She's on duty today."

"She said she didn't have time to talk to civilians." Mam had the grace to look slightly guilty for already talking to Deputy Olivia Washington, one of Marietta's great-nieces. "But I know they're getting the sheriff's department boats together at the landings, and that they called the Coast Guard."

"There's going to be a run on the Pig." Bonnie sounded worried about the island's only grocery store, a Piggly Wiggly whose business boomed in the summer. "They always restock on Mondays, which was why I was waiting till this afternoon to get hot-dog buns for supper."

"I've got some. Y'all can eat with us. Lindsey, too."

"Thanks. Now that we know where our next meal is coming from, can we finish this tomorrow morning? I need to get to Pinckney. Did you tell the Roes?"

"Yes." Bonnie gestured toward them. "Ricky's going to help me dump our stuff after they get cleaned up and put a tarp down. They can't do anything else until Otis gets here."

I started back toward our plot, but Mam stopped me. "Look across the fence. Do you see it?"

"See what? A bird, a plane . . ."

"That fluffy yellow bush behind where that tree's come down." Mam pointed. "I think it's a Lady Banks rose."

"Don't they bloom in the spring?" Bonnie craned her neck.

Mam was already hoisting herself on the fence for a better view. "Some bloom later. I want one for the arbor out back. The deer don't like them, and they climb like crazy. Come help me get a specimen."

"You sound like you're at the doctor's office." Bonnie grimaced. "And you will be if you get in that poison ivy back there."

"I'll be careful. Lindsey, give me your gloves. Mine are in the car." She took her floral knife out of her back pocket.

"Do you want clippers? I'll go get them."

"No, I just need you and Bonnie to boost me over." She was clinging to the metal fencing like a spider monkey.

"Better idea, sis. We can all get over where this tree limb fell on the fence." Bonnie was scrambling over the oak branches as if we were kids again playing with my brother, Jack, in the backyard.

"Wait up, Tarzan." I stepped over an old grave marker to the tree's uprooted base. "This must have just come down in that last storm."

"What's this?" Bonnie picked up some kind of metal chain caught knee-high in a scraggly branch. "It's a necklace—no, look, dog tags." She wiped them on her overalls and squinted. "I can't read the print, though."

"Let me see." Mam's arm reached over my shoulder.

"Watch out! This tree branch is slick." I could feel my foot sliding. "And there might be snakes."

Mam stopped suddenly and overcorrected her balance, making me lose mine. With dizzying speed, I was sprawled on the spongy earth, my mouth and nose pressed up against dirt and leaves and who knows what.

"Lindsey, are you okay?" Bonnie was crouching over me. "Mam, be careful. You're going to fall, too. Lindsey, say something."

I raised my face off the ground and twisted my neck. "Get off my hand." My voice came out in a croak.

"Oh, sorry." Bonnie shifted, and I tried flexing my left hand. My fingers still worked.

"Anything broken?" Mam this time. "I'll help you up."

"No, stay there." I rolled over on my side and then my back, wincing as something sharp poked my spine. I looked up at Mam, silhouetted against the light blue sky. "You want to put up the knife?"

"Oh, I forgot about it. Good thing it was in my other hand. I might have stabbed you."

"Something did." I sat up, leaning against the rough charcoal bark of the limb that had been my downfall. I took off my sunglasses, which had smushed into my nose. Then I reached behind me and ran my hand gingerly over the mat of forest primeval until it grazed the rock I'd been lying on.

Only it wasn't a rock.

"It's a ring," Bonnie said. "A high-school ring."

"What's it doing on that stick?" Mam leaned over to see better.

"It's not a stick." I closed my eyes, then opened them again. "It's a bone. A ring finger."

CHAPTER FOUR
Headlines and Deadlines

"How many fingers am I holding up?" Mam made a peace sign in front of my nose.

"Two." I swatted away her hand. "I don't have a concussion."

"There's a red bump on your forehead that looks like it's going to bruise. Either that or you're getting the world's largest zit."

"I bruise easily. I'll probably look like I've been in a wreck."

"You already do. Are you still dizzy?"

I shook my head. The world didn't spin. "It's just the heat. I stood up too quick when Randy and Ricky came."

"Probably." Bonnie sounded concerned. "It's like the time we were in the antiques store in Wilmington last summer. One moment you were looking at the jewelry fine as could be, and the next you had keeled over on a settee."

"And Mam never did get to the bargain place next door." I drank some water and then held the plastic bottle to my forehead. Mam was right. I did have a goose egg. "That settee had icky green and yellow stripes."

"You must be all right if you remember that, but just sit here on the bench. Stay in the shade. We'll go see what's happening. If you're okay, that is." Mam was ready to abandon her role as nurse now that I was upright.

We all looked across the Colonel's plot to the fence, where the

Roe brothers were crouched by the uprooted tree. Ricky appeared to be combing through the dirt and layered vegetation where I had fallen. He stopped and said something to Randy, who shifted a leg-sized limb to one side and peered underneath.

Bonnie screened her eyes from the glare so she could see better. "I wonder if they've found more, uh, more . . ."

"Bones?" Count on Mam not to mince words. "Of course they have. It's a cemetery."

"But it's not *in* the cemetery," Bonnie noted. "It's on the other side of the fence."

"That doesn't mean anything. At least I don't think so. The grave was probably there before the fence, although it seems like whoever built the fence would have found it back then. But maybe not if it was under the tree and that was the boundary." Mam was thinking and talking at the same time. "Maybe it's more than one person. Maybe it's another really old graveyard, like the slave cemetery in the woods at Pinckney or the Indian burial mound under all the oyster shells—"

"The ring, Mam," Bonnie interrupted. "It was a high-school ring."

"That could just be a coincidence. Somebody lost it over by the fence."

"Attached to a finger?"

Bonnie's challenge stopped Mam momentarily. "Well, there is that."

Randy walked toward us, automatically avoiding any graves. "It's not superstition," he'd said earlier, "just being respectful. Sometimes, you can't help it, though." He looked a lot like his younger brother, but the gap in their ages was carved on his weathered skin. "How you doing?"

"Fine," I said. "A touch of the sun. The water helps."

"We've got more in the truck. This weather, you need to drink a lot."

Mam couldn't stand it any longer. "So, it's a grave, isn't it? I bet this happens all the time, right? You dig a new grave and find an old one."

"Not really." Randy frowned. "Not like this."

"Like this how?" Mam, of course, but we all wanted to know.

"Without any sign of a coffin, for one thing. But still buried deep enough that animals didn't get to it and scatter the bones. If the tree roots hadn't brought 'em up, they'd still be there and none the wiser."

"Do you know how long it's been there?" Mam asked. "Or do you have to call in forensics?" She's a big fan of crime shows on television.

"We'll call the sheriff. We would anyway. Coroner will have to see everything." He reached in his pocket and pulled out the ring we'd discovered. It had fallen off its owner when Mam had insisted on a closer look. "But this is a clue, for sure. Granville County High, 1969. I was class of '67, so I probably know her."

"Her?" Bonnie asked.

"It's a girl's ring." Randy held it out on his palm. "Initials R. C. B. Should make identification pretty easy. Of the ring, anyway."

"So these dog tags I found don't belong to the body?" Bonnie held them out to Randy.

He was surprised. "You didn't show me these."

"There hasn't been a chance since Lindsey fell and then practically passed out. I forgot about them." Bonnie was apologetic. "They were tangled on a branch by the fence. Or maybe it was a root. But they weren't wrapped around anybody's neck bone."

"Can you read them?" Mam asked. "We were trying to when Lindsey slipped."

"Because you pushed me." Sometimes, I can't help myself.

"It was an accident." Mam brushed my comment aside to concentrate on Randy, who was scraping away the crud on the tags with a pocketknife. "Well?"

He handed the tags over to Bonnie. "Type's too small for my eyes, and my reading glasses are in the truck."

"Franklin C. P . . . No, wait, that's a B. Bailey. Wasn't that Miss Eliza's husband?"

"No, Marietta said her son was the one in the army." Mam turned and looked over by the Roes' Laramie truck and the Bailey plot. "Isn't he buried over there?"

"No." Randy shook his head. "No, that can't be right. Frank's at Arlington."

"Then he wasn't buried with his dog tags." That seemed logical.

Randy's face was troubled. "His daughter used to wear them."

"Becky?" Mam was disbelieving. "The one who ran off and drowned during Camille?"

"Becky," Randy said, his voice wondering. "I'll be a bluetick hound. R. C. B. Rebecca Comfort Bailey. Becky."

❦

I felt sorry for Fort. Just as Randy was going to call the sheriff, Fort drove up, trailed by Rabbit Hare in a rusty pickup. Fort wanted to make sure the Roes had gotten the news about the bridge. Then he was hit with the news about the bones.

"Becky? Our Becky?" Fort seemed to shrink into himself, his creased face folding like a deck of cards when Randy told him the news. "Sweet Jesus. I don't believe it." He put his hand to his forehead and leaned back against his grimy Land Rover. "No, no. Becky drowned. People saw her get off the bus in Gulfport. It can't be her."

"Can't be," Rabbit concurred. "Becky drowned. Said so yourself." He spat in the dust.

Bonnie flinched beside me even though we had hung back a few feet, unsure of our role in the situation but not wanting to be left out. Rabbit looked even rattier than usual, greasy gray hair hanging in hanks from underneath a faded red baseball cap. Gray stubble on his narrow face, gray chest hair sprouting from the top of a ragged T-shirt that might have once been white but was now, not surprisingly, gray.

"Are you sure it's Becky?" Fort straightened up.

"No, of course not," Randy said. "Coroner will have to determine that. But I wanted you to know about the ring and the dog tags."

"Let me see those." Fort had regained some composure. "Maybe somebody stole them from her." His voice grew more confident. "That's it. Has to be." He seemed to notice us for the first time. "What are you doing here?"

"Yeah," Rabbit echoed, "what are you doing here?"

Mam was unfazed. "We found her. Back there by the fence. I wanted a Lady Banks rose, and Bonnie found this gap in the fence where the tree fell, and then Lindsey tripped or slipped and landed on this stick, only it was a bone. . . ."

She was still talking as Fort strode past her, heading for the site. Rabbit was right behind him, and I smelled old sweat and rank river mud as he went by. Bonnie flinched again.

The Roe brothers exchanged glances. Ricky followed Fort and Rabbit, while his older brother turned toward his truck.

"I'm going to go call the sheriff," Randy said. "Got to be at least one deputy this side the bridge."

"Do you think it's Becky?" I asked.

He stopped. "Yeah, I do. There never was a body. I'm the one put in that memory stone for her, next to the one for her daddy. She never took those dog tags off. Fort knows that."

"Maybe someone did steal them." Even Mam seemed doubtful.

"Be a helluva coincidence." Randy's brow furrowed. "The dental records will tell. And then the sheriff can figure it out."

"Maybe she went to Mississippi and came back for some reason," Bonnie speculated.

"Maybe." Randy's eyes shifted toward the back of the graveyard. "Maybe she never left."

※

The switchboard left me on hold for what seemed like an eternity. At least I was in air conditioning. Picking up a cell signal as soon as I turned toward Pinckney and the river, I'd parked in a shady spot off to the side of the crumbling blacktop.

"This better be good, Lindsey," R. W. Hampton growled in my ear. "I got a paper to put out. Holding the front as it is. You got some new angle on this bridge mess?"

"Nope, but this is just as good, maybe better." I plunged straight in. "Remember Becky Bailey?"

R. W. paused, then said, "Yeah, went to high school with her. Long brown hair, wrote poetry, was in Drama Club. Drowned during Camille, poor kid. Never found her."

"Until now."

His questions came like bird shot. "When? Where? Dead? Alive? Who else knows?"

"No one yet, but Randy Roe's calling the sheriff now." I quickly recounted the morning's events.

"Hot damn, Fox. Nobody's going to hear about bones in a cemetery on a scanner and think there's a story there. You got us a scoop, girl. I won't call AP till after we go to press. Heck, I won't call 'em till after the eleven o'clock news. It'll be too late for Charleston's and Columbia's regional editions. How fast can you write it?"

"Me?" It had been years since I'd written hard news on deadline.

"Who else? I gotta go see if I can up the print run. And rip up the front page. And track down what's-his-name, Dustin, at the bridge and tell him to get a move on."

"If you're talking about the new guy, his name's Justin."

"Whatever. He puts his own byline on everything, even the crime log."

That reminded me. "No byline for me."

"Why not? 'By Lindsey Fox. Special to the *Times*.'"

"No. 'Compiled from staff reports.' Or put your name on it, Mr. Editor. And you're going to have to get Justin to call the sheriff's department for a quote."

"Oh, crap, I forgot your conflict of interest. You sure?"

"I'm sure." I didn't want any story coming between me and Will. "I told you when I said I'd do the history column. No sheriff's department. No drug busts. No crime."

"I know, I know. If you're gonna cover the circus—"

"—don't get cozy with the elephants," I cut in.

R. W. chuckled. "Something like that. Hey, I'm going to give you to the desk so you can dictate."

"Dictate?" Even when I was doing hard news in Charlotte, I had rarely written on the fly.

"You bet. It's 'Hello, sweetheart, get me rewrite time.' I'll call you if I have any questions after I read it. Keep your cell on. Hang on, I'm going to transfer you."

I was on hold again. I sang to a Muzak version of the Beatles' "Yesterday" while I flipped through what I'd scribbled in the notebook I kept in the car. Old habits die hard. I could feel some of the same adrenaline I'd heard in R. W.'s voice. To outsiders, we probably sounded callous—media hounds on the trail of trouble or misery or scandal. Actually, it was the part of the job I'd hated most, intruding on private tragedies for public consumption. What I liked was putting the pieces together, choosing the right words, and telling a story. Also the serendipity of it all, people and places and events coming together in unexpected but satisfying ways. Features were fun because you could play with the formula required by hard news—who, what, where, when, why, the inverted pyramid, the lead, the nut graf . . .

"Lindsey?" R. W. again. "Everybody's tied up. I'll take it. Start talking."

"Okay, but don't interrupt me and try to edit me as we go." I could picture R. W. at the computer, shirt sleeves rolled up. "Wait till the end and then we can figure where you need to fill in."

"Yeah, yeah, I know what I'm doing. Let's hear it."

I took a deep breath. "First graf. 'Hot summer, comma, cold case, period.' New graf. 'Workers on Indigo Island made a chilling discovery Monday morning when they found the skeleton . . .'"

CHAPTER FIVE

Scoops and Snoops

" 'Hot summer, cold case.' " Bonnie put down the copy of today's *Centerville Times*. "I like it. You certainly got the *hot* part right. I'm about to melt."

"Me, too." I lifted my hair off my neck. "Literally." Upon coming into my blessedly cool office at Pinckney, I'd immediately felt a trickle of moisture down my back. Outside at Miss Eliza's service, I'd been "glowing," as Nanny used to politely put it, noting that "men perspire and hogs sweat." Now, I was starting to drip. The ceiling fan was clicking so much on high speed it sounded as if it might take off.

"I don't get the *cold* part," Mam said, plopping into the old armchair crammed in one corner. "I mean, they're pretty sure it's Becky, right? Those were her belongings. It's just a matter of formal identification. They'll get one of those forensic pathologists, like Kathy Reichs, the *Bones* writer. One of her books was set down here in the Low Country. Maybe they'll get her."

"She works out of Charlotte," I said. "And she's a forensic anthropologist. A pathologist does bodies, anthropologists do bones."

"We've got bones," Mam said. "Assuming they're Becky's, they're just old, not cold."

"But she didn't jump in the ground by herself." Bonnie sat back on the narrow window seat and kicked off her sandals. "Think, Mam. Somebody put her there. Plus, how did she die in the first place? She disappeared almost forty years ago. That's a really cold case."

"Another suspicious death." Mam nodded. "How come we keep getting involved with dead bodies?"

"You make us sound like necrophiliacs!" Bonnie exclaimed. "And we are not involved, at least not so anyone knows."

"Yeah, how come we're not in the story?" Mam looked at me. "You made it sound like the Roes found the grave."

"Do you want CNN camped on your doorstep?" I asked. "You saw the cameras outside the gates at the cemetery. Once the bridge got fixed, the bones became the story. R. W. told me he was getting lots of calls because Fort wouldn't talk to any reporters."

Mam took the paper from Bonnie. "Who's this 'source close to the investigation' who said Fort appeared stunned by the discovery and had identified the 'personal items as having belonged to his niece'? Or did R. W. put that in? How come he didn't say who?"

I grinned. "You know reporters don't reveal their sources."

"Did you talk to Olivia?" Mam looked puzzled. "She wasn't there. How does she know about Fort? And why are you snickering, Bonnie Lynn?"

"Because I'm the source, silly. I wasn't going to let Lindsey use my name."

Mam turned to me. "How did she get to be 'close to the investigation'?"

"She was right there on the scene."

"Well, so was I! How come I didn't get to be a source?"

"You can be a source next time," I assured her. "If you climb a tree, I'll even call you a 'high-level source.'"

"Pooh!" Mam looked at the paper again. "I thought you said you weren't going to write any more about it."

"I'm not, at least not really. R. W.'s going to take over. But he wants me to do something on the Comfort-Bailey family curse for my history column next week. The stuff Marietta told us. I'll talk to her some more, and Miss Augusta, too."

"Miss Augusta did not look good at the cemetery," Bonnie said. "Is she not feeling well?"

"She told me she had a headache and was going to lie down this afternoon," I said. "She hasn't had much sleep, and Miss Eliza was her good friend."

"But she looked more upset today," Mam said. "I hope all this hasn't been too much for her. She could have another spell. I better go check on her."

"Marietta's already gone. She'll let us know if there's anything." I pulled the tour-guide schedule out of a pile of papers leaning precariously on my desk. Both Mam's seventeen-year-old daughter, Cissy, and her best friend, Ashley, were on duty this afternoon. "I'll tell Cissy and Ash to steer the tourists away from the Coach House. It says, 'Private, No Entrance,' but there's always somebody who thinks that doesn't mean them."

"Don't look at me like that!" Mam stood up. "Just because I got the Employees Only confused with the Ladies at the Publix in Charleston last week. That was an honest mistake. I'm not a snoop. Okay, I am sometimes, when it's necessary. Like now."

Bonnie looked alarmed. "What do you mean, Mam? Marietta will look after Miss Augusta. Oh, no, you don't mean Becky Bailey, do you? Remember what happened the last time you started poking around in a suspicious death. We could all have been killed."

"That was different," Mam said. "That was here and now. You said yourself this is a cold case. Besides, look at this picture of Becky Bailey in the paper. Don't you think she looks sad and serious? Maybe she had a premonition she was going to die young."

"Maybe she was worried she wouldn't have a date for the prom." Bonnie rolled her eyes. "Hand me the paper and let me see."

"I don't see how either one of you can tell anything from a black-and-white thumbnail lifted out of a high-school yearbook,"

I said. "She's got straight, dark hair parted in the middle, and that's about all you can tell. Why do you think she looks sad?"

"She's not smiling." Mam frowned at me. "I'm sure it's the Comfort family curse. She knew she was doomed. See, Bonnie, Lindsey does need our help researching."

"Not if you're going to make assumptions based on an itty-bitty picture. We'll have to find out more about her—get a copy of the yearbook, for starters."

"She said *we*, Bonnie!" Mam crowed.

Bonnie looked heavenward again. Then she did a double take. "Did you know there are some old yearbooks up on that top shelf?"

"Where?" Looking up, I spotted several Granville County High School yearbooks with their distinctive emerald-green bindings. They were stuck in among some old ledgers, a two-volume set of *The Complete Works of William Shakespeare*, and a well-worn copy of *Alice in Wonderland*. As yet, my management duties at Pinckney had not required I consult any of the books, although I sometimes felt like Alice. " 'Curiouser and curiouser,' " I said now. "I have no idea why those are up there. What do you think the chances are of one being from 1969?"

"Won't know till we look." Mam was moving her chair into position under the shelves. "Bonnie, you're the tallest. If you stand on the arm, I bet you can reach them."

"If I don't break my neck." Bonnie stood on her tiptoes, clutching a lower shelf with her left hand while her right fingers played along the edge of the high shelf. "How close am I? I can't tell because I'm smushed up against the wall."

"To the left." Mam waved. "Right."

"Which is it?" Bonnie leaned against the shelf for support, turning her head toward us. "This is not as easy as it looks."

"To your left," Mam said. "You're almost there. Warm, warm, getting hot—there, on fire!"

Bonnie grasped at one yearbook, but it was tightly packed in with its fellows. "There went my last good nail. Drat!" She gave another tug and teetered backward as the book suddenly came free.

"Look out!" I called, but too late. As Bonnie stumbled to her knees into the seat cushion, the falling yearbook crashed to the floor, missing Mam's head by inches.

"Lawsamercy!" Marietta was standing in the doorway. "What's this commotion? Sounded like the roof fallin' in."

"Just me!" Bonnie grinned from the chair. "And this yearbook I was getting from the top shelf. What year is it, Mam?"

"It's 1967," she said, dusting it off. "Maybe 1969's there, too."

"Should be," Marietta said. "Julia had her a collection."

"How come?" As far as I knew, Miss Augusta's late daughter had never gone to Granville County High, attending boarding school in Richmond. Besides, she would already have finished high school, maybe even college, by 1969.

"Julia teaching at the high school that spring in 1969." Marietta's face darkened. "Before the summer she ran off and broke her mama's heart."

"Really?" Mam said. "I thought she died in 1971."

We all knew that Miss Augusta's only child had been killed in a car wreck in Canada, having run off with her draft resister boyfriend. Her army colonel father had been furious, cutting off all communication between his rebellious daughter and the family. Julia had died before Miss Augusta could bring about a reconciliation, and then her husband had a stroke not long after. She had returned to Pinckney and shut herself up in the dilapidated plantation house for months on end before finally emerging as the stalwart Miss Augusta we knew, renovating the family home and turning Pinckney into a tourist mecca. Forget *Steel Magnolias*. Miss Augusta's spine and spirit were forged of some stronger metal— titanium or tungsten.

"Julia gone two years before then," Marietta said. "Everybody in that family stubborn as mules. It hard on Miss Augusta not seeing or hearing from her all that time, and then she gone for good." Marietta shook her head. "Maybe that why she feeling bad.

Them finding those bones remind her of the last time she had Julia."

"Was Miss Augusta at Pinckney that summer?" Bonnie's tone was gentle. Marietta was clearly upset by the reminders of Julia, too.

"No, they at the war college that year. Julia here by herself, but I come see to the house like always. Sometimes she here, sometimes she not. She was at the high school till after dark most days, helping out with the yearbook and the drama."

"Did she teach English?" That would explain the books on the top shelf.

"Yes, she loved to read, that girl. Always had her head in a book. She finished at the university early, but she was going back in the fall. Then off she went with that hippie boy." What might have been a tear appeared to glisten in one eye as Marietta sighed. "Long time ago." She turned away. "Lemonade in the kitchen when you finish in here."

"Thank you, Marietta."

"Thanks." Bonnie echoed Mam.

"We won't be long," I called out.

"You didn't ask her if she knew Becky," Mam said.

"It didn't seem like the right time. I'll wait a couple days, especially with Miss Augusta. I didn't realize that was when Julia ran off."

Bonnie clambered up on the chair again. "Let's see if I can find 1969. There should be pictures of both Becky and Julia. Here, catch!"

Mam caught the yearbook this time. "Yippee, 1969! Very good, sis." She hurriedly thumbed through the pages. "Adams, Anderson, Bailey—here's Becky. It's the same picture as in the paper, just a little bigger. She's still not smiling."

I took the yearbook from Mam and looked at the rows of young faces. "She's not frowning, though. She has kind of a faraway look. But it's hard to tell. Except for the hairstyles, all the girls look pretty much alike."

Bonnie's turn. "I see what you mean. A lot of the girls have flips. There are even some of those beehive helmets. Looks like the sixties took their time getting to Granville. Some of the guys have longish hair and sideburns, but most of them are clean-cut. Heavens, they all are so, so . . ."

"Young," Mam supplied. "They could be Cissy and her friends. The hair isn't even that different, at least with the girls." She flipped to the front of the book. "Oh, wow, here's Miss Fishburne. She really looks young, too. Get a load of those harlequin glasses! She must have just started teaching because she retired either last year or maybe the year before." Mam pointed to another picture. "So that's Julia. She looks even younger, like she could still be a student. Her hair's long like Becky's. Do you think she looks like Miss Augusta?"

I brought the page closer. "Maybe. Or maybe like that miniature of Miss Augusta's mother. They all had dark red hair."

"How can you tell in black and white?" Bonnie took the yearbook. "I've never seen a picture of Julia."

"I think her father tore them all up or threw them in the fire. Seems like Aunt Cora told me. But you have seen Julia's picture. She's the one helping Mam and me find Easter eggs when we were little. The snapshot's in my baby book."

"You have the memory of an elephant," Mam said. "Does Miss Augusta have any pictures of her?"

"Just one that I know of. Julia's about ten, I guess. She's got it in a silver frame next to her wedding picture."

"Forget Julia," Bonnie said. "We need to look for more pictures of Becky."

"For someone who wasn't interested in finding out more, you sure are eager now," Mam said. "What are you going to tell Tom about getting involved in another mystery?"

"I'm not going to tell him anything." Bonnie's face was mutinous. "Like you said, this is a cold case. We need to go through this yearbook and see who knew Becky who's still around."

"Good idea. Hand it to me. I know more of who lives here

now. I'll read out names, and you can make a list. I'm thinking, too, we can look tomorrow at the estate sale at Comfort's End for anything that might have been Becky's. We need to get there really early."

February 20

I had to get up early to help Grandmother polish the silver today. We were in the dining room and it was freezing, but Grandmother wouldn't light the heater. She said it wasn't that cold and to put on a sweater. This whole house is cold. Cold and old. So is the furniture. I don't care if they are antique, the chairs are ugly and uncomfortable. Horsehair. I guess it's real. I don't want to think about it. I had to go outside and see if there were any camellias left so Grandmother could put them in the blue-and-white bowl. It was warmer outside than inside! I would have stayed longer, but I heard F.'s truck coming up the drive.

CHAPTER SIX

A Little Dish, or
Early Birds Get the Blue-and-White

The sun wasn't even up as I pulled out the gravel driveway, but who am I to know when it rises? I hadn't been up this early since, well, Monday, when Mam had insisted we go to the graveyard. For that matter, she'd called at dawn the last two days to tell me to turn on the TV so I could see Indigo on the news—the bridge, which had been repaired in less than twenty-four hours, and the bones, which continued to fascinate. Both days, I had gone back to sleep until the dog and cat insisted I attend to their needs. This morning, they both were surprised as I when the alarm went off. Doc had moseyed down the front steps to take care of business underneath a star-spangled sky, and Peaches hadn't had time to push his empty plastic dish off the counter before I filled it with his kibble. At least I think it was his. Otherwise, he'd wolfed down some of Daddy's granola.

I had a granola bar in my book bag for later. Right now, my contacts were keeping my eyes open while I waited for my breakfast Coke to kick in. A truck with a boat hitched to it was in front of me as I drove over the short causeway across the marsh. Somebody else was getting an early start. I yawned loudly. It *was* still dark, for land's sake. I wasn't a dedicated junker or antique buyer, unlike the cousins, who thought nothing of getting up in the middle of the night for a good garage sale. I did like looking for old stuff at antique malls and thrift stores, but they were open at reasonable hours.

Besides, where was I going to put anything? Since returning to Indigo, I had been playing musical houses—a couple weeks at Mam's, then renting from Miss Maudie until she and her family took over Middle House for the summer, now parked in my old room at my parents'. I missed my spacious duplex in Charlotte, which had been taken over by a professor from nearby Queens. A lot of my belongings—heavy on books, dishes, and a few pieces of good furniture—were in storage, waiting for me to settle someplace. I didn't need anything from Comfort's End.

"Need has nothing to do with it," said Mam, for whom the hunt was as important as the quarry.

"It will be the sale of the year!" Bonnie promised.

Even Miss Augusta had chimed in yesterday afternoon. "Now, girls, I know Eliza wouldn't like strangers gawking over all her treasures and mementos. She really should have made other arrangements—a private sale or a bequest to the historical society. Still, you must respect her and buy some of her lovely pieces. She would want them to find nice homes on the island."

What were they, orphans to adopt or something?

"And it's nice and early, so you'll be able to come to work on time," Miss A. had added.

But of course. With so little sleep, I'd have to be careful not to snarl at the tourists, whom Miss Augusta insisted on calling "guests." She and Walt Disney would have gotten on like a house afire, although she was appalled when she heard an island girl had chosen to wed at Cinderella's Castle instead of Pinckney Plantation. "Well, I never," she'd sniffed. "How tacky."

I yawned again and drank some Coke. The sky was finally turning light. A slight breeze was blowing. Maybe it wouldn't be so hot, but I had my doubts. June already had broken heat records, and now we were heading into July and August and some of the sultriest days of the year. I slowed as an otter scurried down the road in front of me, as if to say, "Hurry up, hurry up. There's a long line." It spoke with Mam's voice.

"Maybe you could put some stuff at Will's," she'd suggested when I bemoaned my homeless state. "Since Jimmy has moved back to Columbia, he's all by himself. And he's not even on Indigo now. You could—"

"—not go there," I said. Trying to keep my cousin from minding my business was like trying to stop the tide from coming in. Useless. Still . . . "His place isn't that big, plus he needs a new A.C."

Will rented an old beach house that had been relocated from the sand to a far less desirable lot on a side street. It wasn't so much a fixer-upper as a falling-downer. But Will faced the same problem as other islanders who had seen property values on Indigo skyrocket in recent years. It was getting so those of us who had grown up on the island no longer could afford to live here if we didn't already own something. Then there was Fort Bailey, land-poor but still trying to live rich. Comfort's End, indeed.

I braked for the turnoff to the old house. A convoy of cars, SUVs, and pickups already was parked on the huge side field that might have once been a lawn. Whoa, there was a long line to get in the house. Mam was up near the front, of course, and yes, Bonnie was right behind her with Sally Simmons.

My watch said 6:03. How did they do it? Shoot! People were holding numbers. So much for cutting in with the cousins. I took No. 18 from a dapper bald man I didn't recognize who was standing sentry at the front walkway, which was missing more than a few pavers. No. 18—well, I was in the second group. Bonnie had said that only ten would go in at a time. I sighed. This just wasn't me. I'm taking this Coke can in, I told myself, gulping again. No one was taking my caffeine!

In front of me, two mothers with babies in strollers chatted away. The babies were asleep, or at least quiet, in their deluxe chariots, all comfy cozy. Nets for mosquitoes and gnats and everything. I yawned again, then scratched my leg in the damp grass. Eliza's yard was pretty shot. A red rose bush straggled over an old brick fence next to a couple of sago palms, but that was about it for landscaping. The area had been recently bush-hogged for parking, I guess, but it still felt buggy. How long before they let us in? One of the stroller babies cried out, and a pacifier went in. Why in the world would you bring a baby to an estate sale? Then again, when you're up early with a baby, you might as well go somewhere, and shopping would be good. Nothing else was open at this hour. Maybe if you didn't wake the husband, you got to spend more money. Sounded fair to me. I continued to scratch.

Uh-oh, we were moving. I waved to the cousins, but they didn't notice as they stampeded to the screen porch. Nos. 11 through 20 waited with me. What had Bonnie said, fifteen-minute intervals? Maybe it was just five. The other baby started crying. No pacifier materialized. Rats. I tried to block out the wails as I concentrated on all the cousins had told me. What was it they wanted me to look for? The partner's desk for Bonnie. Mam was hoping for some floral frogs, whatever those were. They didn't look like frogs, though, she'd said. In real-estate lingo, a FROG was a "front room over garage," or maybe it was "fourth room over garage." Whatever. I couldn't afford it. I wasn't sure how far my pennies would go at this estate sale, for that matter. Blue-and-white china, which we were all mad for, varied in price as much as pattern.

The cranky baby quieted, and I was able to catch a little of what the moms were saying—something about "blue cobalt." Then they lowered it to a whisper as they glanced behind them.

At me? Were they really looking at me? Blue cobalt? Well! The challenge was on! I better go straight to the butler's pantry. Couldn't let these two beat me to the blue-and-white! The line moved. The screen door was opening for our group. I looked at my Coke; suddenly, I needed free hands. I poured out the remaining liquid, then slipped the empty can into the back tray of the closer stroller and casually trotted past the Mommie Dearests. They were struggling to push their infant cargo in the cut grass. Ha!

She travels fastest who travels alone. As I headed down the long entrance hall, bypassing the crowd in the living room, I could hear the cousins in the kitchen.

"I love this still-life painting," said Bonnie.

"Me, too," said Mam.

"Oh, and look at these old recipe books," said Bonnie.

"I like those, too," said Mam.

"I think I'm going to buy some of these old linens," said Bonnie. "This embroidery is exquisite."

"I want those, too," said Mam.

"For Pete's sake, Mam, look for your own stuff!"

If I hadn't been hurrying to stake out my claim, I would have stopped to tell them exactly how ridiculous they sounded. But the stroller brigade wasn't far behind.

There! A built-in china cabinet with glass doors. One was broken, so I just reached in and grabbed two cobalt blue salt and pepper shakers, along with a beautiful blue-and-white English sugar dish. It was pricey, with an "ND" sticker on it.

"What does ND mean?" I asked the bald guy who had been handing out the numbers and was now officiously hovering at the dining-room entrance.

"No discount," he answered with a know-it-all attitude. He tried to look snooty but was too short—not much taller than me—to carry it off successfully. Probably had a Napoleon complex.

"Thank you," I said graciously, and received a supercilious smile in return. Napoleon the jerk.

I should have remembered "ND" from the cousins' crash course in Antiques 101. Bonnie had said, "Don't pay the asking price, unless it's a no-discount piece." Naturally, my items were marked ND. I reluctantly put back the sugar dish. Oh, well, I was happy enough. Kind of like hunting for buried treasure. I pawed through a brown box stacked with dishes to see what else I could find.

"Those are pretty," said Bonnie, swinging though the pantry door, arms piled with lots of linens.

"Mmm." I hovered over my potential finds like a mama hen.

"Well," Bonnie fussed, "the partner's desk is gone! And so are most large pieces, though Mam bought a vanity bench *and* everything else I admired. I was holding out for that desk, so she just kept picking up everything I said I liked. I can't believe my sister!"

"I can," I said, although I knew Mam would gladly give Bonnie her pick of anything she had bought. Maybe not gladly. They did seem to have the same taste in things like that and often wore the same colors at the same events. I always wanted a sister. My brother, Jack, who was three months younger than Bonnie, had been a pest when we were growing up, although now we managed to get along most of the time. "I like that old tablecloth. It reminds me of the one with the red cherry clusters that Mama used to have. Sorry about the desk."

"Maybe the family is keeping it. I'd ask Sally, but she's disappeared. I saw Fort a little while ago talking to his appraiser pal, Gibbs Henry, and then he went out back toward the barn," Bonnie said. "I'm going to go see if I can find him."

"Is there stuff for sale back there?" I asked, suddenly greedy for more.

"Don't know, but I'm going anyway," said a determined Bonnie. "Don't tell Margaret Ann." She gestured back toward the front hall. "You pay Gibbs for what you buy."

"Who's Gibbs?"

"The appraiser, I told you."

"I know, but who is he, what does he look like?"

"Short, bald."

"Napoleon complex."

"Yep. That's him. Remember not to pay—"

"—the asking price, I know, I know. But so far, everything I want is ND." I was hoping I sounded like a pro, but Bonnie turned and headed out the back door, not really caring about my new expertise.

Maybe there was good stuff in the barn. But I still hadn't finished in here. Not that there was much to choose from. The plates I'd been looking at were all chipped and/or stained, as worn out as the house itself. The wood floors were warped in places, the finish long gone. Window sills were crumbling, and there were cracks in the plaster. Dust was everywhere. Underneath the grime of the ages, the house still had good bones, but this sad old belle needed more than a facelift. Calling *Extreme Makeover*.

A brown carton on the old marble baking slab caught my eye. Something was sticking out the top. A fan! The kind made of cardboard with a paint stick for a handle. It took me back in time—Nanny in white gloves fanning me as I lay in her lap on a worn pew. It could have been the same fan, "Indigo Baptist" written across the bottom, Jesus and lambs on one side and a white church on a hill on the other. Over at Fishing Creek Methodist, where I went with the Fox side of the family, we'd had fans with the Last Supper. I pulled another fan from the box. This one said "Hiott Hardware" and had a large-antlered buck on it. Wait, what was that under the tissue paper? Dishes? Plates? They were wrapped in crumpled, yellowed tissue, but I saw blue-and-white. Before I could investigate further, Mam suddenly appeared at my side.

"Ooh, blue-and-white!"

"Mam!"

"What?"

"I got dibs on this box," I said hurriedly, remembering what happened with Bonnie.

"I'm *just* looking," she said. "Anyway, I'm spent out. I allow myself a certain amount. Of course, I go over it every time. I found the neatest white vanity stool to maybe use on my new porch, and some linen to recover it, some old recipe books, and two floral frogs!"

I looked into her nearly empty canvas bag.

"Oh, I've already put my stuff in the car. But I kept my book on blue-and-white. Let's look up some of this stuff and see how close Fort was in pricing it. I bet Gibbs Henry helped him."

"I'm sure he did, and then tacked on more."

"Oh, look at this!" She pulled the first piece from its tissue before I had a chance. "Hold it while I look it up," she commanded, handing me the china. "Here it is. It's a footed bowl—Dickens?"

"Dickens?" I echoed.

"Yes, scenes from Charles Dickens's stories, the magazine illustrations. It's 1840 and worth $268 without the cover! It's beautiful! I bet he'd take $100."

"Are you insane, me pay $100 for a bowl?" I exclaimed.

"Shh. Okay, maybe try $50, in which case you could end up paying $75. It's Ridgway," Mam whispered, reading her book. "It would make a gorgeous centerpiece with white hydrangeas in it. Can't you just see it?"

"I can see that it's too much," I said. "Let's look at the plates." I started unwrapping them. "Pretty. It's a scene of a castle." I flipped it over. "Enoch Woods Castles Dalguise, 1929. It's $35. I could get that."

"It's not in the book," said Mam, "Offer him $5. Oh, I like this one! Spode, Aesop's Fables, 'The Lion in Love.' It says it's worth $360! Ugh."

"Fort's price is $350 ND. Hand me that other one. It has a hairline crack, but I like it. I could bake cookies and serve them to company."

"You, bake? Company? Ha! Who? Will? He could care less if his cookies are served on heirloom blue-and-white. You'll need to display this."

I ignored her comments about my hostess abilities and looked again at the beautiful footed bowl.

Mam sighed as if giving in to a child wanting candy in a grocery store. "Okay, I can put $25 toward it and count it as your birthday *and* Christmas. Y'know, like our mothers always do. But you must let me use it for a Christmas dinner centerpiece and any family wedding luncheons I give."

Hmm. I caught the wheel of a stroller out of the corner of my eye "It's a deal." I quickly put it in Mam's bag.

"Take your stuff in my bag, but give me my price book. I'm going to find Bonnie. Remember, don't give him the asking price if you can help it. Where'd you say my sister went?"

"I have no idea," I lied, and then felt guilty. "Maybe out back? Thanks for my birthday present."

"And Christmas." Mam headed for the door. "And you're welcome."

The outside air was a welcome relief from the stuffy parlor, where the early buyers crowded around the cashier while Gibbs checked off their purchases in a thick ledger.

"It says ND—no discount. This is not a garage sale," he told one freckled-faced woman trying to get him to knock twenty-five dollars off an orange knitted afghan so hideous I wouldn't want it in my house.

Still, one woman's trash was another's treasure, and within fifteen minutes, I had my footed bowl, my slightly cracked plate, and my cobalt blue salt and pepper shakers. My bargaining skills had paid off—I got the bowl for an amazing sixty dollars, the S&P set for ten, and the cookie plate for five. I also sprang for a Jesus church fan for fifty cents!

I wanted to show my stuff to Bonnie, but first I needed to sit down. Going around the side of the house, I found a moss-stained stone bench under a dogwood tree. Old slate pavers peeked from underneath the overgrown crabgrass. Maybe this used to be a path to a garden. I wondered if a young Becky Bailey had ever sat here, or even a young Eliza. Indigo was such a past-haunted place. These gnarled trees bearded with moss had been here for generations, witnesses to who knows what. For that matter, so had the things I bought. Who had first admired the English bowl? Had it traveled to Indigo aboard a ship, perhaps as a present for a bride? Funny, how objects lived on long after their creators and owners. But that was part of their allure. From elegant antiques to cherished family heirlooms, each had a story. But many tales could only be guessed at. I thought of Becky's high-school ring with its fake emerald and shivered despite the heat. Somewhere, someone was walking across my grave. . . .

A familiar voice interrupted my thoughts. Bonnie must be around the corner of the house. I started to go warn her that Mam was looking for her, but just then I heard her say the name Becky. So I waited. Then another voice, lower, male. Fort, maybe.

"So you read the story?" Bonnie must be coming in my direction because I could hear every word now. "Did you know Becky in high school?"

Obviously not Fort.

"Sure, the school was pretty small," the anonymous voice replied. "I remember we were all shocked when she was lost in Hurricane Camille the summer after graduation. At least that's what everyone thought. Now, I'm not so sure."

"I know," Bonnie said. "Some things don't make sense to me. Like, how come her mama's family in Mississippi didn't call Miss Eliza when she didn't show up?" Bonnie's trained mind was covering all the bases.

We had tossed that question around the last two days among ourselves. The stories I'd found in the newspaper's morgue weren't as detailed as we'd hoped. The passengers of the Greyhound bus Becky supposedly was on had taken refuge from the hurricane in a local church, only to have the whole sanctuary wiped out in the ensuing storm surge. There were no survivors, and only a few bodies were recovered. It was assumed Becky was one of the missing.

"Communication wasn't so 24/7 back then," the male voice commented. He sounded familiar, but I couldn't place him. "You had the network news and the papers, but there was no cable showing all the chaos and destruction. Could be her Mississippi kin didn't have a phone, and the power was knocked out. Took awhile before anyone knew Becky wasn't where she was supposed to be. Say, you want to go crabbing with me sometime this week? I expect Ben and Sam would like it."

Wait. Who was this person who knew Bonnie's boys?

"Would they ever!" Bonnie said. "I hope they didn't totally disrupt Bible school last week."

Okay, he was a Baptist. Who had Bonnie told me was helping out with the classes this year? As soon as I heard him laugh, I knew. Wayne Jenkins. My dentist. My very nice-looking dentist. Careful, Bonnie. Wayne was a widower whose practice included practically every woman in Granville County. Although, to give him credit, he was popular with men and kids, too. Or as popular as a dentist can be.

"Crabbing would be fun," Bonnie said, rounding the house but looking back over her shoulder. "You can call me at Mama's."

She was walking right past, so deep in thought—and with a smile on her face—that she didn't see me under the tree.

"So, Bonnie, a date with the dentist?" I inquired. "Wayne the incredible hunk?"

Startled, she dropped a shoebox she was carrying. "Lindsey, it's not a date! Those boys are so busy, he knows I need help with them since our daddies aren't here." She started gathering up the spilled items from the grass.

Yeah, right. She was looking down, so I couldn't see her face, but the top of her ear was red. Sunburn or blush? I wondered if I should say more about Wayne. He didn't look as old as he was—mid-fifties, I think. Even though he had gray hair, there was lots of it, and he was naturally lean. He fished with Will and J. T. sometimes, and Daddy said he was a good golfer. He was seeing a woman in Beaufort, but Aunt Boodie heard they broke up because she wanted to get married and he didn't. And of course, he had good teeth.

"Here, I brought you this box of old costume jewelry. It's only two bucks," Bonnie said. "Maybe the tour guides can find something suitable to wear. Either way, it should be fun to pick through. You know, the brides now are pinning decorative brooches to their bouquet stems. Mam will probably want some. Anyway, take it to Pinckney with you." She plopped the flimsy box—which originally had held a pair of ladies' Papagallos, size 7—down on the bench and looked back to where she had left Wayne.

"By the way, in the barn back there, which is locked up tighter than Fort Knox, there *is* lots of furniture. All NFS—not for sale.

Fort said it was going to a private dealer in Charleston. It's really a shame 'cause I saw what looked like a partner's desk and an old icebox, too, when I was looking through the window."

"Those windows are up high. How could you see?"

Bonnie turned red. "Uh, um, Wayne gave me a boost."

I raised my eyebrows. She couldn't hold my gaze. I took pity on her. "Want to see the blue-and-white I adopted?" I proudly displayed my purchases.

"Those are nice," said Bonnie. She passed the cracked plate back to me. "So, you really think Wayne is a hunk?"

I rolled my eyes and handed her my Jesus fan. "I think you need this."

My watch said 7:58. I was tired already, and now I had to go stand in line again and pay for the junk jewelry.

March 10

I am so tired of not having enough money to buy nice things. Grandmother is so stingy. She never comes out and says it, but I always feel like I am a charity case. It's not my fault I'm an orphan. I didn't ask to live with her. I liked Mississippi and living with Mama's cousins, even though they really are poor. Francine said I could stay but that Grandmother really wanted me to live with her, and that I would have more opportunity because Grandmother has money. Grandmother only has money because she never spends it, unless it's something she wants or F. says he has to have. The only opportunity on this island is when I get to leave it for college. She will pay for that because it is her "duty" to my father. She didn't like my mother, she thought she was trash. My mother was not trash, even if she did work at Woolworth's and liked a good time. We had fun, and she liked nice things and pretty shoes like I do. I have dark hair like her. Grandmother hates my hair. She was blond, and so was my father. I don't remember him, but I have seen the pictures and I have his dog tags. I told Grandmother I used my measly allowance to buy my Papagallos, and they were on sale. J. gave them to me. She said they were too tight for her. But I think they fit her fine, and she said that so I wouldn't feel bad about taking them. I wish I was pretty like Mama or J.

Chapter Seven

Sunset Cruise

Bonnie reached for the line wrapped in a figure eight on the dock cleat and yelled back over her shoulder, "Hurry up! We only have forty-five minutes of light left!"

I could hear Mam trotting down the wooden planks. The tide was so low the dock house loomed above the boat, where I was already settled in admiring the tan on my outstretched legs. I hadn't been out in the sun for ages, but Jergens Natural Glow lotion gave me the smooth color I'd longed for as a teen. And no smearing like with tan-in-a-can.

"Did you remember the wine and the shrimp dip?" asked Mam, who had suggested this diversion at the estate sale this morning. I yawned—a sunset cruise had seemed like a good idea at the time—and patted the cooler beside me.

The boat shifted and dipped as Mam stepped in. She grinned as she dangled a key from her finger. "J. T. doesn't have a clue about hiding things. I know all his secret places. Anyway, he'll never know we took it for a short spin while he's at the land-trust meeting. Let me get it cranked up before you untie us." She turned and hollered, "Come on, dogs!"

Chloe and Doc, who had been sniffing something on the grassy bank, scampered down the ramp. Doc, the retriever mix, immediately leaped on board, heading for the bow, while the tubby black-and-white cocker shared my forward seat. Mam gave Bonnie the go-ahead, and she pushed off and stepped on the bow in one swift movement, joining Mam behind the wheel. Mam drove while Bonnie directed. I yawned again as we slowly eased down the creek, J. T.'s white boat sleek and stark against the chocolate brown pluff mud and dark green water. The hum of the motor underscored the early-evening chorus of insects, birds, and frogs. No mosquitoes yet, thank goodness.

The peace didn't last. Mam, of course. "Y'all rushed me so, I didn't have a chance to tell you what I found in my bench I bought at the estate sale. It was crammed up under the top. I started ripping off the old upholstery that smelled really bad, kind of like—"

"Short version, Mam," Bonnie interrupted.

"Okay, okay. It's a notebook, and I think it might have been Becky Bailey's because the cover's got that sixties pop-art look."

"Which is back in style, along with peace symbols and hiphuggers and a lot of other clothes," I said. "Where is it?"

"In my carryall."

I pulled out the composition book with psychedelic purple and orange swirls and circles on the cover. The pages were almost full of curvy handwriting.

"It's like a diary or journal," I said, opening it at random. "There are entries and bits of poetry. Here's some Edna St. Vincent Millay: 'What lips my lips have kissed . . .'"

"If you're going to read goopy poetry, I need wine," Bonnie said. "I'll get it and the food, and you can continue with the teen angst. Is it really Becky's?"

"It's got her name on the inside cover: 'Becky Bailey. English 12, third period.'"

"Maybe she wanted it to look like class notes, in case anybody saw her writing in it," Mam suggested. "Give me that Sprite. I'm driving."

"About two miles per hour." Bonnie handed Mam the green can. "I suppose you want me to fix you some crackers, too. Go a little faster, the gnats are starting to bite. Blast! One just landed in the shrimp dip! Lindsey, keep Chloe out of the crackers."

I glanced over at Mam, who just shrugged. Bonnie was sure moody these days. "This isn't all goopy. Here's 'No man is an island,'" I read. "Then this is her: 'I don't think John Donne ever lived on a real island like Indigo. You are cut off from the rest of the world if you don't have a car or a boat. I hate riding the bus to school. Last year, I rode with R., but there wasn't anybody this fall, so I couldn't do anything after school. I was supposed to be secretary of the French Club. Thank goodness for J. Now I can work on the yearbook.'"

"I hated the bus, too," Mam said. "It took forever, and we were the first on and last off."

"But you and Lindsey always sat together, and I got stuck with Jack." Bonnie shuddered.

"At least he was a cute boy."

"He was my cousin!" Bonnie waved a cracker in indignation. Chloe thought it was for her. "Down, dog. Mam, didn't you give her any supper?"

"Doesn't matter," Mam said. "Back to Becky's diary. I wonder who R. and J. are. We'll have to look at that list we made from the yearbook. Ray Simmons was on there. I'll go by the real-estate office tomorrow and see if I can get something out of him. You didn't get much out of Wayne, Bonnie."

"But she's going crabbing with him," I said. "So there's another chance."

Mam looked at her sister with surprise. "You didn't tell me that."

"He's taking the boys." Bonnie's voice was prim. "I'm just along for the ride."

"Well, good. See what else he knows. I've got an appointment week after next, but it's just for a cleaning. Hard to ask questions when your mouth's wide open. Dentists are bad about that. They talk and ask you questions, and you can't answer."

"Sheer torture for you," I chided. "This dip is good. Whose is it?"

"Paula Deen, I think," Mam said. "I don't think it's Rachael Ray's. No EVOO. Why is olive oil extra-virgin? Is it ever just virgin? I used extra cream cheese in this."

"Still de-lish." Bonnie drank from her plastic cup. "So's the wine." She walked back to check the depth finder. "Tilt the motor up a little. It's only two feet deep here." Looking up, she pointed down the creek. "Hey, it's so low we can explore past the causeway bridge. I've always wanted to see that part of the creek."

"Is the tide coming in or still going out?" I asked. "We don't want to get caught on the other side of the bridge with not enough room to go under."

"We're okay for a while," Mam replied as we passed into the shadow of the bridge.

Chloe barked and hovered against my leg, and Doc barked just before he flattened himself on the bow, like he was ducking to go under the bridge. The sounds of the motor bouncing off the concrete pilings and water reverberated eerily.

"I'm putting this diary back in your bag," I said. "It's getting too dark to read."

"Yeah, I'm going to need the flashlight." Bonnie began calling out depths. "Two feet . . . Now three . . . Now one and a half . . . Now six. Look at the fish in that deep hole." She tapped the finder with her finger.

"Remind me to tell J. T. about that spot sometime. If I tell him tonight, I'll have to explain we were out. But Daddy and Uncle Lee will want to know, too, about another good fishing hole." Mam expertly followed Bonnie's signals. "I hope they don't bring us any salmon from Alaska like J. T.'s friend did last year."

"Why not?" I said. "Salmon's wonderful. Cook it on the grill or poach it. Mama's dill sauce. Mmm, mmm, good."

"J. T. only likes fried fish. It was pretty bad."

"You *fried* salmon?" Bonnie was aghast. "For the love of Pete. If they bring us salmon, we'll let Aunt Mary Ann cook it. Whoa, it's getting shallow. One and a half."

Now I remembered why we never came down this way. Too

nerve-racking, always wondering when the mud flats would finally grab the hull and hold on for dear life. Just when the creek seemed to end, it curved around a mound of marsh grass, and the water opened up a few feet before bending again. It was like a Southern version of *The African Queen*.

A marsh hen squawked, protesting the invasion of her sanctuary. Startled, I sat up a little straighter. Doc and Chloe went on full alert, noses high, ears pricked. "Look." I pointed off to the left. "There's a light up under those trees. I didn't know there was a house out here."

Mam stood up on the boat bench to look over the spartina. A fringe of tall pines was silhouetted against the dull gold of the darkening sky. "Probably an old fish camp. I wonder what road it's off of."

Bonnie climbed up to look. "If not for the light, you would never notice the place. Except for the dock, if you want to call it that."

The oyster-shell-encrusted pilings spiked upward, but the dock itself was snaggle-toothed where planks were broken or completely missing. I didn't like the looks of the place. "Let's turn around. It will be completely dark soon. See, the tide is coming in, and we want to be able to get under the bridge."

Mam was still staring at the light. "Do you think you get there by Middle Tree Road?"

"You can explore by daylight sometime." Bonnie stepped down. "Lindsey's right about the tide."

Doc sat at my feet. Or rather on them. He gave a little whine, and Chloe snuffled beside me. They were ready to get a move on, too.

Mam carefully maneuvered a turn in the narrow creek, tilting up the motor a little more. It felt like we were dragging on the bottom. Then the boat slowly eased forward. The dark had descended amazingly fast. Bonnie didn't have to look at the depth finder going back, since the tide had come in, but she directed the beam of the light ahead of us. We had on the boat's running lights, but going back was still slow.

"The bridge should be around the next turn," Bonnie said.

I could see a set of car lights going by on the road ahead. A dark mass appeared beyond the running lights. "There it is. Can we still get under?" I asked doubtfully. There was a gap of only about three feet between the water and the underside of the bridge.

"Good grief, I don't want to scrape J. T.'s boat." Mam sounded worried. "Nope, I don't want to even try it. Gosh, it sure seemed that tide came in fast. It must have already started coming in when we went through the first time."

"Well, what are we going to do now?" demanded Bonnie. "I don't relish keeping the mosquitoes company for the next six hours until the tide goes back out. I told the Hendersons I'd be back before too late to pick up the boys. It's so nice they are keeping their grandson this month and like having Ben and Sam over. I don't want to take advantage."

"Well, we'll just have to go back to that dock at the fish camp and tie up. If I walk out to that road, I'll probably be able to tell where we are, and I can call Cissy to pick us up," reasoned Mam. "Then I'll come back early in the morning and get the boat and bring it home safe and sound."

She turned the boat around. No one said anything. Mam was probably trying to figure out what she was going to tell J. T. And who knew what Bonnie was thinking these days? The night air was thick; the slight breeze had disappeared. The landscape—or what could be seen of it—looked different, almost ominous. I heard a whine near my ear and slapped at my neck. Vampire mosquitoes. Where was the bug spray?

"It's in my bag," Mam said, even though I hadn't spoken a word. Cousin telepathy. I passed the plastic bottle to them. "There's the light. And here's the dock. Bonnie, put out the bumper so the boat doesn't scrape against the post. J. T. will see the tiniest mark."

Bonnie tied us up. "How are we going to crawl across the walkway with the dogs? It looks like it might all fall apart."

Mam's flashlight played over the broken ladder and the rails connecting the pilings. Maybe it would be better to drive the boat up close to the bank and try to jump. Of course, if we missed, we would land knee deep in pluff mud and probably lose our Crocs in the process. Then who would be left to tie up the boat? I sighed. This was not going to be fun.

"Bonnie, you go first," Mam prompted.

"Gee, thanks." If anybody was going to fall, it would be Bonnie. She really is a klutz.

"Watch out for loose boards and nails sticking up," Mam warned.

"Well, shine the light over here 'cause I can't see a blasted thing!" Bonnie swore under her breath.

As soon as I stood up, Doc decided not to wait. He scrambled over the side of the boat into the shallow water and went up the bank. "Doc, wait there!" Now he was going to need a bath before bed. Well, we could both use the outside shower. I was sure to be filthy after this little adventure.

"Here, put Chloe's life preserver on her." Mam handed me the doggie jacket. "We might have to carry her over the rickety spots."

Oh, joy. Cockers are not easily carried, especially fat ones. Their legs just swim about in the air as you lug them along.

Bonnie called back, "Come on, it's not as bad as you think. There's just one bad spot in the middle. Here, Mam, hand me the light."

Before I could protest, the light flew right over Bonnie's head and into the creek. Swell.

"Good toss, Mam." Bonnie was getting testy.

"Sorry. I have another one." Mam the cheerful Girl Scout. "See?" She clicked on the second flashlight and shone it in my eyes. "Here, Lindsey, hand me up Chloe."

I wrapped my arms around the reluctant dog, grunting at her weight as I hefted her toward Mam.

"Good girl."

Did she mean me or Chloe?

"You can have a cookie when we get home."

Obviously, she meant the dog, who needed more treats like I needed more mosquito bites. Forget cookies, I was going to need Benadryl. And tweezers for the splinters in my knees. Doc greeted me with a shake as I hauled myself up off the dock. "Good dog. No lick."

We followed Mam up the path, stepping around busted crab traps and other rusty fishing paraphernalia. The outside light was a flood, lighting up the unpainted shack and the clearing around it. Old oyster shells crunched underneath our feet in the remains of the dirt driveway. No one appeared to greet us. The place was deserted.

Mam couldn't resist a chance to snoop, though, and stepped up on the slanted porch. "Let's look in the windows. Hey, you two, come see if you can see anything." She stuck her flashlight up to the window. "Never mind. There's some stuff in there, but I can't tell what it is. Furniture and boxes. Somebody must be using it for storage. I think I would have heard if anybody was living out here."

"Come on, Mam," Bonnie said impatiently. "I'm tired."

"And I need help corralling these dogs," I added, a hand on each collar. "We don't want them taking off into the woods."

Bonnie grabbed Chloe, who stubbornly pulled her toward the bushes.

"Let's go!" Mam headed up the rutted driveway, which would supposedly lead to the main road.

"Do you have your cell?" I called after her, suddenly remembering her bag was still on the boat.

"It's clipped right here to my pants pocket. Come on, Bonnie. I guess I'll have to swear Cissy to secrecy about this little boat snafu." Mam started punching the cell phone as she headed up the drive. She looked up and stopped as we reached a wider dirt road. "Oh, hey, I know where we are. It's not that far from the house, as the crow flies." She shook the phone. "Why isn't this working? We're close enough to the bridge to get a signal."

Bonnie looked at me. "There were truck tire marks back there in the sand near the shack. But I didn't see a truck."

"Me either. But I wasn't looking for one. Mam has the flashlight."

"Heck, this phone is dead as a doornail," fussed Mam. She sounded just like her mother. The parents have a hard time with cell phones. "Let's walk this way. The main road's up there." She pointed at the darkness in front of us. "We'll cross it and go down, and we'll hit my road, and then on to my driveway. Piece of cake on my road." She picked up Chloe. "Oh, Bonnie, shouldn't you go back and get the cooler out of the boat? The coons will be all over it tonight."

"No way!" Bonnie snapped. "We've only got one flashlight." She grabbed the light from Mam, shone it in front of her, and started walking.

Gee, this was going well. "I brought the bug spray," I said.

"Pass it here." Bonnie didn't even say please.

We continued in silence. The road was overgrown with scratchy weeds that poked at my ankles. Myrtle bushes reached out to grab us, and water oaks arched overhead. Somewhat surprisingly, Doc trotted contentedly at my left side, my fingers hooked loosely under his collar.

"I can't keep carrying you, Chloe," said Mam, setting the dog down. "C'mon, you can keep up. That is, if Bonnie wasn't walking so fast." She called out, "We can't see back here!"

Bonnie didn't reply but slowed her pace.

Mam was undeterred. "This reminds me of camp and having to get up in the middle of the night and hike to the latrine. I was always so scared there was someone lurking in the woods, like the guy with the hook for a hand in that ghost story."

"Thanks for reminding us." Bonnie waved the beam forward. "There's a streetlight. Unless it's the ghost with the lantern looking for his head." She stopped suddenly. "Did y'all hear that?"

"What?" Mam whispered nervously.

"It sounded like a stick or a twig breaking." Bonnie directed the flashlight behind us. Nothing.

I felt a prickle of uneasiness. "Trust me, if there's anything or anyone, Doc will let us know."

At that very moment, I felt the fur rising from his back as he gave a low growl.

Bonnie squeaked and took off running. So did Mam and even fat Chloe.

I gave Doc's collar a tug. "This way, boy." He resisted for a fraction of a second, then we ran after the others, his leaps threatening to dislocate my arm from its socket. But I didn't dare let him go. He might run across the paved road, where even now headlights were whizzing by.

We were all winded as we stopped under the streetlight.

"Let's cross," said Mam.

I glanced back once. Was that movement in the woods? My imagination? Or maybe a deer? I didn't think so. In that split second before we'd fled, my nose had picked up a distinct smell in the humid air.

Cigarette smoke.

March 21

We are meeting in the cemetery tonight to celebrate spring. R. will bring smokes, and J. will bring wine or beer. I am taking some RC because I think beer tastes sour. It reminds me of F. I can smell it on him. He makes me sick. J. says ignore him and he'll go away. I wish. He can't go in the army like his Citadel pals because he has a heart murmur that they found when he went for his physical. He doesn't want anybody to know he's 4-F. He tells people he can't go because he is supporting the family as the only surviving son. He's afraid people will think he's a peacenik or a sissy. He goes hunting all the time because he likes to kill things. Lots of men hunt, but it is different for him. I've heard him talking to his gun.

CHAPTER EIGHT
Where There's Smoke

The first time Mam smoked a cigarette was also the last. Her eleven-year-old face turned green, and she started hacking so hard I thought her eyeballs would fall out. Taking my cue from her, I only pretended to inhale, holding the smoke in my mouth briefly before trying to blow a perfect ring like our cousin Danielle. Four years older than me and Mam, Danielle was the one who had handed out the Salems and matches. We thought Danielle was very cool, even glamorous. She lived in Florida and came to visit twice a year, wearing the latest trendy fashions out of *Seventeen* magazine. She had long, polished fingernails and fabulous Farrah Fawcett hair. She had a boyfriend. We wanted to be just like her.

"I still blame Danielle for getting me started smoking," I told Mam now as we drove back to the fish camp. Here I was up at daybreak again. This had to stop. "Why couldn't she have been addicted to something healthy, like aerobics or flossing?"

"You both finally quit," Mam said, brushing the crumbs of her breakfast muffin off her blue Citadel T-shirt onto the passenger floor of my CR-V. "So did our daddies and J. T. and practically everyone we know. Are you sure it was cigarette smoke?"

"Oh, yes, definitely." Even though I had no intention of ever picking up a cigarette again, I still found a whiff of smoke initially seductive. Then I would remember how hard it had been to quit—Danielle's suggestion of cinnamon sticks as a substitute never really cut it—and the impulse would pass. Filthy habit.

"Slow down, there's the turnoff. Boy, you wouldn't know it was here unless you knew it was here."

I understood Mam perfectly. A short break in the jungle of vegetation by the side of the dirt road, a veiled parting in the curtain of green, was the only sign of the overgrown drive to the camp. "Good thing we're high up. I'm not sure you could get through in a regular car."

"It seemed farther last night," Mam said as we jounced into the small clearing. "Spookier, too."

I opened the car door to a soggy blanket of air. "It's just as hot, though. Are you sure you want to go crabbing? Maybe you could just get the boat and I could go on to Pinckney." Or I could go home and go back to bed.

"Forget it. This is supposed to be your morning off, and I've got Cissy taking care of the gift shop. She didn't complain one bit."

That didn't surprise me. Since Cissy had broken up with Will's son, Jimmy, at Easter, she'd been playing the field. The latest entry was a college student whom Posey had hired to help with the outside stuff at Pinckney. Cissy and Stephen were studiously ignoring one another whenever Mam was around, so I knew she wasn't ready yet for her mom to start the interrogation as to his qualifications and intentions and to ask the inevitable "Do we know his people?" Since Stephen was working today, no doubt Cissy was thrilled at the opportunity to be at Pinckney without her mother helicoptering nearby.

I yawned. "I didn't think it would be this hot so early."

"It'll be cooler on the creek, and I'll put the top up." Mam slammed the car door. "You're the one who wanted to go crabbing."

"Sort of. When Bonnie said she was going with Wayne and the boys, I started thinking about how good it would be to have some crab cakes. But I was thinking more in the abstract. Y'know, like how when I think of blueberries, I think of going to get some at King's Market, and you start pulling out pails for the you-pick-'em place. You did say you'd clean the crabs." Mam knows my aversion to the ickiest part of crabs.

"Yes, but you have to help pick out the crabmeat *and* tie your own chicken necks to the lines. It's not like live bait." Mam surveyed the tumble-down shack with its rust-stained tin roof and grimy windows. "It doesn't look quite as bad in daylight."

"You think?" I thought it was worse, all sad and neglected. I looked at the ground to see if I could find any of the tire tracks Bonnie had claimed were here last night. Or any cigarette butts. The toe of my blue Croc scuffed the dirt and bits of gravel and grass. Nothing unusual. I couldn't even tell where we'd trod in the dark. Not enough bare earth to discern any prints.

Mam headed down to the remains of the dock. "I was thinking last night when I couldn't sleep that this is a nice piece of property. I tell you, I tossed and turned for hours. I planned funeral flowers for people who aren't even dead yet. Let me check the boat and then we can snoop around a little." She scooted across the broken board as if on a jungle gym.

"What are you looking for?" I asked, watching her navigate the holes in the dock.

"My bag—I still can't believe I went off without it—and the cooler."

"I meant up here in the camp."

She didn't hear me, she was so busy rummaging around in the boat. "Here's the depth finder, and the cooler." Of course, I could hear her. "Where's my tote bag?" she wailed. "It's missing!"

"No, it's not. What all was in it?"

"The notebook, the crackers, and the rest of the shrimp dip." She looked up at me. "Really, it's not here. Do you think coons could have dragged it off?"

Coons could yank off seemingly secure garbage-can lids. A Triscuit box and a Tupperware container wouldn't stand a chance.

I hoped they hadn't tried to wash the tote bag. Becky's diary would be gone forever. There was no sign in the marsh, though, of a faded red-and-tan Land's End tote bag monogrammed *MAM*.

"I swear, Bonnie could have gotten it for us," fussed Mam, coming back up the bank. "We had our hands full with the dogs."

"Let's look around in the back. Maybe a coon did drag it off."

"Or a person. I think there was somebody watching us."

I looked around uneasily. Something more than just the sunlight was different from when we'd been here before. Wait, that was it. "Look, Mam, the floodlight's off! Either it burned out or—"

"—someone has been here." She grabbed my arm, her eyes wide. "Maybe they're still here!"

"Where?"

"In there." Mam dropped my arm and marched up the rickety steps to the shack's poor excuse for a porch. Taking the end of her T-shirt, she rubbed the window nearest us and peered in.

"Can't really see," she said, moving from window to window.

"I'll try." On second thought, ugh, spiders. I stayed behind her, cautiously looking over her shoulder at the smeared glass.

After knocking loudly on the front door and twisting the locked knob, Mam turned to face me. The screen door slammed shut behind her with a bang. We both jumped.

"Okay, so no one's here," she said. "But here, hold still. There's a spider on your shoulder."

"Where?" I danced around in a tizzy, shaking my head and brushing off my arms. "Is it gone? Did you get it? Are you sure it's not in my hair? Mam! Mam?" Why wasn't she answering me?

"Right here, Lindsey." Her voice had climbed an octave, and she had clenched my arm again.

"Mam?" Maybe she had seen a snake. I opened my eyes and followed hers. The front door was opening.

"Hello, Rabbit," Mam said a tad shakily. "We didn't know anyone was here."

Rabbit stared at us, his eyes beady behind the limp strands of gray hair.

"Our boat couldn't . . . ," began Mam.

"I know all about your boat and the tide and your stupid fat dog. She peed on my house," Rabbit sneered.

"Your house?" Mam asked. "You live here?"

"None of your business." It came out like "bidness." Rabbit not only looked like a character out of *Tobacco Road*, he talked like one, too. Judging by his stained fingers and teeth, he also smoked. "Now, get off my property 'fore the tide turns."

That seemed like a good idea, but Mam was having none of it.

"Not until you give me back my tote bag."

Did she have X-ray vision?

Rabbit spit. Yuck. "You can have it. That dip weren't no good." He reached behind him into the shadowed interior and picked up the canvas tote. "Come get it." He held it up by one dirty finger.

"Thank you," said Mam, quickly moving up the steps. She snatched the tote bag and looked inside as she hurried back across the unpainted porch. She nodded at me. Good. The diary was safe.

Rabbit saw her. "Them crackers were stale, so I put 'em back. You might want to throw them away."

He could bet on that.

"I'll go help with the boat, and then I'll come get my car," I said.

"Don't care what you do, so long as you leave and don't come back. You best stay away from the graveyard, too. Digging where you shouldn't be. I knowed better than to go back there by the fence."

"It's not your cemetery," Margaret Ann started, but I interrupted her.

"What about the fence?"

"Nobody knows more about that place than me," Rabbit boasted. "I knows things. Secrets. Mr. Fort trusts me. He lets me live here."

"This place belongs to Fort?" Mam asked.

Rabbit grinned. Not a pretty sight. He wasn't one of Wayne's patients. "Bye, now." He disappeared inside, slamming the door.

"I'm sure he's still watching us," Mam muttered.

"Yeah, but you're getting in the boat. I've got to come back by the shack to leave. Give me the tote bag."

Mam handed it over. "Okay. Wait, though, 'cause if I can't get under the bridge, I'll have to come back again."

"I'm *not* waiting, and you *will* get under that bridge, Margaret Ann, if you have to lie down on the floor of the boat and steer with your foot! Call me on the cell. I'll be in the car waiting up by the first turnoff. As soon as you're under the bridge, I'll drive to your house." I can be bossy, too, when need be. I did wait for her to climb in the boat and crank the motor before hurrying to the car. As I pulled out the drive, I looked in the rearview mirror. Rabbit was out on the porch again. Good thing looks can't kill. Otherwise, Mam would have been fixing my funeral flowers. Roses, I'd told her once before when I had the flu. "No carnations. Tacky."

I got to the house before Mam, giving me time for a needed bathroom break. Then I put the tote bag in the hall closet, first pulling out Becky's notebook. I really wanted to read it now. Could R. be Rabbit? Surely not. I reluctantly slipped it into a plastic bag and put it in a tray in the refrigerator. Unless a lunchmeat thief was on the loose, the diary was safe underneath the bacon. I'd have to tell Bonnie—Miss BLT herself. She'd get a kick out of my hiding place.

Going down to Mam's dock to wait, I tried to make sense of it all. What did Rabbit know? Or was he just trying to show off?

I could see Mam in the distance. I grabbed the crab lines and nets. She had been lying earlier—she already had the chicken parts tied on. And there was a cooler of ice with PB&Js and bottled water and a Coke for me and, yes, more blueberry muffins. She had probably done it all at five-thirty this morning, but hey, I was grateful.

"Don't talk yet." I held up my hand. I could see she was bursting to say something, but we needed to get settled first. I handed off the cooler and crab lines and climbed in. "Remember, we only have until noon. We have to be clean and back at Pinckney at one-thirty. I brought a change of clothes—"

"Listen, listen," she interrupted. "On my way back, I saw what looked like a U-Haul truck hidden up in the woods this side of the camp. It must be Rabbit's."

"Why would Rabbit have a U-Haul truck?" I was skeptical, knowing that Mam often makes death-defying leaps of logic. "He has a pickup."

"I don't know, maybe it's busted," Mam said. "We didn't see any other cars or trucks at the camp."

"We didn't go around in the back, and there weren't any tracks."

"We just didn't see any. They could have been there, and Rabbit could have swept them away."

"Rabbit with a broom?"

"Okay, but then who does the U-Haul belong to?" Mam asked stubbornly. "I did see it. You can't miss that orange in the daylight. It was probably there last night, too, just like Rabbit. You have to admit the whole situation's a little fishy."

"So are these crab lines," I said. "Let's get going, and then we can talk."

"But—"

I put my hands over my ears. "La-la-la-la," I sang. "I'm not listening."

Mam grinned, and I could see her gums flapping, but then she attended to the boat. Soon, we were both lost in thought. But it was hard to think of dark and deadly things while on the creek. It was so alive this morning at low tide. The sunlight shimmered on the water, catching flashes of silver as menhaden jumped in front of the boat. I could even see tiny shrimp popping near the bank and minnows swimming in frenzied circles. Perhaps they ran from something bigger.

Mam slowed and dropped the anchor in the mouth of a smaller creek. Gulls folded their wings and settled in to watch, calling out raucously. A marsh hen splashed and then swam to hide in the green spartina. Fiddlers scrambled about over the mud flats, in and out of the coon tracks, waving their big claws. Rush hour on the creeks, and this was one busy interchange.

Mam handed me two lines, chicken parts and a weight tied in the center. You only had to drop them in and wait. The nets were just for dipping. Simple, really, this old-as-dirt way to catch your supper. I hooked the lines around fishing-pole holders, one on each side of the front of the boat. Mam had hers on each side in the stern.

She broke the silence. "I have to hold at least one of them. I like to feel it when the crabs start nibbling. Oh! See?" She slowly pulled in the line she was holding and lifted two large blue crabs over the side, flipping the net in one graceful motion and dumping them in the bucket. "That's two, let's keep count," she said.

"Right, now back to Rabbit." I kept an eye on my lines in case a crab was looking for a snack.

"And Fort. Maybe it's his truck. If you can believe Rabbit, it's his camp. But do we really think he knows some secret about the cemetery? Maybe about Becky's grave?"

"I don't know. He's been around forever, always gave me the creeps. I don't even know how old he is. Fifty, sixty, seventy? He might not be as old as he looks. But I know he wasn't in school with us. I'm guessing mid-fifties at least. I don't remember seeing him in the yearbooks, though. Then again, I wasn't looking."

"He could have dropped out." Mam pointed to one of my lines. "Check it. It's moving."

How could she see that? I fingered the string and felt a slight tremor. "Here's number three." I pulled in another large blue. "He could have been showing off a little. We can tell Bonnie and see what she thinks of this new mystery."

"The real mystery is my sister," sighed Mam. "What in the Sam Hill is she doing flirting with Wayne and going crabbing with him? Has she lost her ever-loving mind?"

"Midlife crisis," I thought aloud. "Tom has been gone for

almost four months. You know it's totally innocent. She just wants some male attention, and he's giving it, and he *is* a looker."

"He's twenty years older than she is!"

"Age doesn't seem to matter. She thinks Stephen is hot, and he's in college. Hormones. Could be she's going coastal."

"Postal?"

"Coastal! It happens all the time in Key West. People come there to escape, and the freedom goes to their heads, and they do crazy things. Bonnie's not working this summer, she's down here without Tom, and now even the parents are gone. She's feeling flighty. Gone coastal."

"Well, Will is gone now, too, and I don't see you flirting with Wayne or Stephen or any other guy." Mam looked at me accusingly.

"Oh, please. He may be cute, but he's not Will," I said. "And I talk to Will almost every night, although I about fell asleep on him last night when we were planning our weekend getaway. Remember, you're working for me tomorrow afternoon and Sunday."

"Where are you meeting?"

"I'm not telling." I quickly changed the subject as I pulled in another two crabs and dumped them in the bucket. "Doesn't Bonnie tell you stuff? Y'all talk all the time."

"She usually tells me everything, that's what's so weird." Mam was aggrieved. "Right now, she's totally oblivious to what she's doing and what it's going to look like if she keeps it up and the island tongues start wagging. Part of it is Wayne's fault, but Bonnie better not put herself in a position to be tempted."

"You sound like a preacher, Mam. Bonnie knows what she has with Tom. I'm sure she wouldn't risk that."

"Well, I'm going to keep a close eye on her and squash any rumors that start. You let me know if you hear anything."

For a while, we pulled in our crabs silently, throwing the little ones back. Gulls dove for some floating chicken that had been pulled loose.

"Sixteen," I said, counting the scuttling creatures.

"Are you going to tell Will about Rabbit?" Mam asked.

"Nope. He still doesn't know we found the grave. He read the wire story, but it wasn't detailed. He's got his own secret mission going."

"The South is full of secrets," Mam intoned. "What do you talk about if not what's going on here?"

"None of your 'bidness.'" I waved the net at her. "Y'know, the South is full of secrets!"

Mam was undaunted. "When Will gets back, you can get some inside info on the case. Maybe Rabbit killed Becky. Or maybe Fort killed her and Rabbit saw it. Could it have just been an accident? How could someone have lived here all this time with that kind of secret? It had to be an accident."

"Pull up your lines, and let's head back," I suggested. "Eighteen total, not bad. Let's go home. I'll get the anchor."

"Such a beautiful sky," said Mam, stretching. "Even if it is hotter than blazes. She started the motor. "Not a cloud anywhere, just that smoke over there. It's way too dry for someone to be burning on purpose." She turned the motor back off. "Do you hear a siren?"

A faint wail was growing louder, although the way sound travels over water, I couldn't get a fix on where it was or in what direction it was headed.

"Must be a fire," Mam continued. "Thank goodness it's north of my house. Maybe a wildfire, someone threw a cigarette out a car window. There's nothing much over that way."

I stared at the rising smudge. "Nothing but Comfort's End."

CHAPTER NINE

Burning Questions, or Too Much Nature

As we got closer to Comfort's End, the smell of smoke became stronger. We were out on the open river, the Sea Fox skimming the light chop, the wind in our faces. The salty air mixed with the sharp scent of burning wood, and a bruise billowed on the blue horizon.

We hadn't hesitated. Maybe it was just a brush fire, in which case we were taking a scenic detour. And if it was the old house, then it was news—more fuel for the curse of the Comfort-Baileys. I hated thinking of that heart pine as tinder, more of Indigo's history lost to elemental forces.

"Too much nature," I said to Mam, which was what we always said when the island's wild side threatened to overwhelm us.

We had coined the phrase after Mam's surprise encounter with a coiled and hissing snake under her house. "It was between me and my flowerpots," she had told me over the phone, sobbing. "I couldn't get to the hoe, but the ax was by the stairs. But just cutting it in two didn't do any good." She hiccupped through her tears. "I was screaming at Chloe to get away. Oh, it was awful! I grabbed this old umbrella and just started beating it over the head. Living on this island! Sometimes, it's just too much nature!"

Now, she looked at me soberly. The last time we'd said "Too much nature" was when lightning had sparked a dock fire on Crab

Creek. The owners were still waiting on permits from the state to rebuild.

"Lightning didn't start this," Mam said, steering us past the old ferry landing toward a weathered dock reaching out in the river. A large Private Property sign was tacked on a rough gray rail, a No Trespassing placard underneath it. Mam was unfazed. "Maybe that's Fort's boat, or else someone beat us here. Anyway, there's room for us. Climb out and tie me to that front cleat."

A smoky haze prickled my nose and eyes. Tall trees obscured the house's picturesque site overlooking where the river widened into the sound. I strained to see if I could spot the chimney. "The sirens have stopped," I said as we went up the rickety steps molded into the bank. "Maybe that's good." We stopped, panting, at the top of the bluff. "There's the house! It looks all right. The fire's behind it. The barn?"

"That must be it." Mam pointed to a grove of oak trees that provided a glimpse of red trucks and blue flashing lights. The wind had shifted away from us, but the smell of charred wood hung heavy in the air. Volunteer firefighters who lived closer to Comfort's End than the island substation had parked pickups and SUVs in the side yard where we had lined up for the estate sale. "Look, there's Bonnie! That must have been Wayne's boat."

We hurried over through the thick grass to an old tire swing. Six-year-old Ben was pushing four-year-old Sam as Bonnie looked on. She heard us and turned, then hurriedly put her finger to her lips. "Shush," she said, moving out of earshot of the giggling boys. "They don't know."

"Know what?" Mam asked. "That there's a fire? I'm surprised they're not watching." She looked longingly at the smoldering ruins of what had been the barn. Small flames still licked at the embers, but the firefighters appeared to be in control. One directed a stream of water from the tanker hose, but several others already had shrugged off their protective black-and-yellow gear and were passing around plastic bottles of water and Gatorade. Wayne was talking intently to Cap Lockridge from the filling station, who was holding his volunteer's hat in one hand and pointing at the EMS truck with the other.

"Is someone hurt?" I couldn't see behind the boxy truck's open rear doors. "Is it Fort?"

"They're giving him oxygen," Bonnie said. "And I think he's got some bad burns on his hands and his back."

"Trying to rescue his mama's antiques?" Mam started toward the action, but Bonnie caught her arm.

"No, it's worse. Rabbit was in there, too."

"Rabbit?" I said stupidly. "He was at the fish camp this morning."

Bonnie's eyes were red. Smoke or tears? "Fort said Rabbit was in the barn when it caught fire. He tried to get him out, but a beam fell on him. Rabbit, I mean, not Fort. Fort was trying to pull him out when the first fire truck got here. He came running out coughing and begging for help, only the roof collapsed right after that."

"What about Rabbit?" Mam sounded stunned.

Bonnie shook her head. "He didn't make it. Wayne came back and told me. They were bringing him out right as we got here. I don't think the boys saw, but that's why I stayed back here with them." She smiled shakily. "They see fire trucks all the time, but they've never seen a tire swing."

"Maybe Daddy can hang one up for them in the backyard." Mam put a consoling arm around Bonnie. "They look like they're having a good time."

Bonnie wiped her face with the tail end of her T-shirt. "They loved being in the boat, too. They're not going to be content just crabbing off the dock anymore. Oh, I wish we hadn't stopped, but we were thinking maybe it was the house."

I nodded. "Us, too. The barn's bad enough. And poor Rabbit." I didn't say it aloud, but I hoped the smoke got to him before the fire. I hated covering fires when I worked for the TV station in Charlotte. The editors loved flames and ordered us to chase sirens whenever possible. An exhibit about Queen Charlotte at the Mint

Museum couldn't compete with video of burning buildings. But the reporter's adrenaline that usually kicked in on a big story deserted me completely when faced with a fatal fire. The smell was stomach churning, its cause horrific.

Wayne came over to us, his face serious. He looked older when he wasn't smiling. "Bonnie tell you?"

Mam kept her arm around Bonnie. "It's awful! What's happening now? Do they know how it started? How is Fort?"

"He's pretty shook up." Wayne started with the last question. "He's refusing to go to the hospital, wants to wait here for the coroner. The fire marshal will work the investigation with the sheriff's department. Cap says Fort was up at the house when he started smelling smoke. Looked out the window, saw the fire, and called 911. Then he remembered Rabbit was supposed to come help him move that furniture he had in there. Could be he was smoking a cigarette, and there were a couple of upholstered pieces that were even more flammable than wood. Fort feels guilty, thinks he should have been able to get him out."

Ben called out from the swing. "Mama, look. Come push us!" He was sitting astride the tire, holding onto the rope. Sam was perched inside the circle, his small, tan arms braced against the sides.

"Hang on!" Bonnie yelled. She loped over to the tree.

Wayne was on her heels. "I'll push."

Mam and I looked at each other. "What do you think?" she asked.

"About what? Rabbit, the fire, Fort, Bonnie and Wayne?" There was a lot to take in.

"None of it's good." She looked at her watch. "Come on. I'm going to see if I can't get Bonnie and the boys to come back with us. You can shower and get dressed for work while I clean and cook the crabs. Then I'll stash them in the downstairs fridge. Cissy will have to hold the fort at the gift shop."

"I'll meet you at the dock. I want to talk to Olivia before we go."

From a distance, Will's main assistant looked cool in her pressed khaki uniform. But I saw the beginnings of a sweat stain as she lifted an arm in greeting. No wonder. This close to the fire, it was hotter than Hades.

"You know I can't tell you anything," she said, her smile taking the bite out of her words. "We don't talk to the press."

"I'm not press today," I said. "And something I want to tell you." I explained about our running into Rabbit at the fish camp and Mam seeing the orange U-Haul. "It doesn't seem to me like there was enough time for him to get over here and smoke a cigarette and just happen to set a fire in the process and wind up dead."

"Mmm." Olivia's smile was long gone. "You might be right. We'll look into it. Thanks."

"Oh, and Olivia?"

"I know. We never had this conversation."

I nodded and headed for the dock and shade. Comfort's End looked sad and desolate in the haze of leftover smoke.

Mam, Bonnie, and the boys were waiting for me on the boat. Wayne held out his hand to help me board.

"See you later," he said as he pushed us off. "Ben, Sam, we'll eat some crabs."

"I no like crabs," Sam mumbled, his bottom lip sticking out. He was sitting in the bow clinging to Bonnie, a couple of tears trickling down his sunburned cheeks.

Ben crowed. "I *love* crabs. They have big claws!" He made a clawing motion at his brother, who promptly wailed.

"Let me guess," I said, being careful where I stepped. "Are they all back in the bucket?"

"I think so." Mam steered us away from the dock. "Be glad you missed it."

Bonnie patted Sam's shoulder. "Sit down, Ben. Let's go, Mam." Her voice rose above the motor. "Too much nature!"

April 12

No moon tonight—dark as pitch. Grandmother goes to bed promptly at nine. TV off. I went out to the tire swing for a while. I do my best dreaming of R. there. I can't believe he is flunking out. He is too smart. J. says he's an underachiever. He doesn't know what he's going to do. His parents are really mad at him. His father says he can't stay at home unless he gets a job. He also told R. he better not be doing drugs. R. laughed when he told us this. He said he was so messed up, and his father couldn't tell! J. and I think maybe he should go to summer school and try again. If he's not in college, he will get drafted. No, no, no! We can't let that happen. He and J. keep me sane. They really listen to me. I feel safe with them. The dark and the mosquitoes chased me into my keyless sanctuary. Sanctuary, ha! That's the ultimate cruel joke. My transistor is under my pillow. I listen as I write by flashlight. WAPE comes in strong, and they play all night. Not too loud, though.

CHAPTER TEN
Southern Charms, or Lafayette Slept Here

"I'm telling you, Mam, it's too much! Cissy is not going to wear a red, white, and blue hoop skirt!"

Bonnie sounded just a wee bit sarcastic to me. I kept my head down, pretending to be absorbed in the plantation paperwork on my desk, while the two sisters argued over how the Pinckney float should look in the upcoming parade. I really didn't want to be involved. The sooner I finished these last bookkeeping chores, the sooner I could head to Charleston to meet Will.

"Well, maybe just a patriotic parasol then," Mam suggested. "Lindsey, where are the big paper clips? This is your copy of the diary."

Bonnie picked up the original notebook from the copier. "Didn't you make me one, too?"

"I figured you and I could read it together this afternoon." Mam efficiently put the clipped pages in a Pinckney purple folder and handed it to me. "I was going to read it last night, but I got sidetracked helping J. T. pack for his mancation."

"Did you really just say 'mancation'?" Bonnie raised her eyebrows. "I thought he was going fishing."

"He is, but that's what they call it these days when a bunch of guys go off together for a weekend. The resorts have started marketing their packages as 'mancations.' They get golf, fishing, poker—all that guy stuff. Cigars instead of fruit baskets. Over at Wild Dunes, it's called 'Dudes on the Dunes.' But J. T. and them are going to somebody's rental house at Santee. They usually go in August, but Harry couldn't go then, and he's the one who gets the house, and this way they get an extra day, and—"

Bonnie held up her hand. "Whoa, I get it. So we can be 'Babes on the Beach,' except we're working for Lindsey."

"Yeah, she's getting her own kind of mancation," Mam snickered. "Like she's going to have time to read Becky's diary."

Bonnie started to say something, but she stopped suddenly and sniffed her hands. "Why do I smell bacon? Is Marietta cooking?"

Ah, food, a guaranteed diversion. I hadn't properly sealed the notebook in its plastic bag when stowing it in the fridge, so now it exuded a faint whiff of Oscar Mayer. Count on BLT to notice. Still, I cut to the chase. "Marietta's made some peach ice cream. Why don't you go have some in the kitchen?" I tried not to sound too hopeful, but I really needed to finish up.

"I think we should all head out to the Coach House and get Miss Augusta's opinion on the parade float," Mam said.

Now, Bonnie was sniffing the air. "Does the peach ice cream have little chunks of peaches in it, or is it the really creamy kind?" Off to the kitchen she went without waiting for my answer.

Mam leaned over my desk. "You know you can't concentrate on that paperwork. So you might as well go with us to talk to Miss Augusta about the float."

I sighed. "Can we at least have some ice cream first?"

We found the plantation owner sitting in her favorite recliner "resting her eyes," as she put it. The Miss Augustas of the world do not nap. Her best friend, Miss Maudie, who was snoozing in another recliner, made no apologies about "dropping off" in the afternoon, but Miss Augusta seemed to regard a need for extra shuteye as a moral weakness. If so, I am an unrepentant sinner. I love naps and had to stifle a yawn on seeing the pair so comfortably ensconced. In Miss Augusta's lap was the shoebox of costume jewelry I had purchased at the estate sale. From the looks of the shiny floral brooch on her lemon yellow pantsuit lapel, Miss Augusta already had picked out something for herself, while pink rhinestones winked behind Miss Maudie's white curls.

Miss Augusta's hooded eyes opened, immediately alert. Of course, she had heard our knock on the door. Now, we were being granted an audience.

"Ah, good morning, girls. You're just who I wanted to see. Please sit down. I have something to give each of you. Maudie, wake up dear. Let's show the girls what we found." She waited until Mam and I settled in the chintz love seat, while Bonnie perched on the notoriously uncomfortable matching wingback chair. Then she reached over to the tea table beside her and picked up three little silver charms off a lace doily. "They're tiny teapots. I believe the historical museum used to sell them."

Miss Maudie announced, "They have them at the museum gift shop," even as she played with her hearing aid.

Miss Augusta raised her voice and enunciated clearly. "That's what I said. Here, Lindsey, yours has lovely miniature filigree on it. So much more appropriate, don't you think, than that creature you wear around your neck?"

I fingered the silver gator charm Will had given me and smiled through gritted teeth. "Oh, how pretty," I said, showing off the intricate carving. "Thank you."

Mam twitched beside me as Miss Augusta turned. "Bonnie, yours has a *C* on one side, for Comfort, I suppose. You'll want to wear it so the engraved side shows. There's a rather too-large rhinestone embedded on the other side. A bit gaudy for daywear, I'm sure you'll agree."

Miss Maudie cocked her head. "Now, I like a little sparkle."

Miss Augusta ignored her as Bonnie nodded and held up her teapot admiringly. Mam twitched again in anticipation.

Miss Augusta bestowed the last charm. "Margaret Ann, yours

is just a darling, round, tubby little thing."

Miss Maudie chuckled. "She said it looked like me. I suppose it does, but I stopped worrying about my waistline a long time ago. Lucky for me, Mr. Frampton liked a woman who looked healthy, and I am that."

Mam cradled the trinket in her hand. "Real silver." She buffed it on her T-shirt. "Imagine it hiding in a shoebox."

Miss Augusta picked up a small wooden box from the table. "Actually, they were in here, underneath these beads and earbobs that we remember as Eliza's." She gestured to her "new" enameled pin. "She used to wear the dogwood in the summer. But I think this cedar jewelry box must have been her granddaughter's, poor child. It's a miniature of a Lane hope chest. Fine furniture stores used to give them away to girls when they graduated from high school. My Julia had one." Her voice faded. I think she surprised even herself by bringing up her daughter's name.

Bonnie and I waited expectantly in hopes more nuggets of Julia's past would be offered up, but Mam interrupted. "Did you know Becky Bailey?"

Miss Augusta blinked as if coming out of a trance. "No, not so I could pick her out in a crowd. She came to Eliza when we were posted at Fort Campbell, I think it was, and I met her once when we came down for a visit. I recollect thinking she'd have been more attractive if she smiled and did something with all that long hair instead of just letting it hang in her face."

"That was the style back then," Miss Maudie inserted. "I remember Eliza telling me Becky rolled it top of her head with an orange juice can. I declare! Imagine sleeping like that!"

"Imagine," Miss Augusta said dryly. "That was the least of it, from what Eliza said. Becky was quite a trial, from what I understand, wasn't she, Maudie? Never tried to fit in, wouldn't even consider making her debut. One of those quiet girls who never have much to say for themselves."

"True, true." Miss Maudie nodded. "She was a good student, though."

Miss Augusta paused as if she were trying to remember something. Her brow furrowed as she continued. "Eliza said she was moody, shutting herself up in her room. They didn't take together, those two, not that Eliza knew anything about raising girls. She spoiled Franklin and Fort to no end, 'bout had a fit when Franklin came home on leave and brought him a pregnant wife. Thought some floozy had trapped her dear boy."

"Oh, it was quite a scandal at the time, as I recollect." Miss Maudie sat up straight in her recliner, her hands tightening on the arms. "Marie—that was the wife, she was a Delacroix from Mississippi, or maybe a Delaroche—had olive skin and dark hair and eyes. I suspect Eliza thought she might have foreign blood in her somewhere, not that she would have said it. But she let her disapproval be known, and there were words. It might have all been straightened out in time, but then Franklin was killed." Miss Maudie sighed. "Oh, that was such a tragedy. Poor Eliza."

Poor Becky, I was thinking. I could tell Bonnie and Mam were in accord. But we were quiet as Miss Augusta touched the brooch that had been her friend's. I wondered if she was thinking again of Julia and words that couldn't be taken back. Still, her tone was neutral when she spoke.

"I didn't see anything in the cedar box that would have been to Eliza's taste, except the teapots. You might find something."

Mam opened the lid, and Bonnie and I leaned over to see the contents.

"Here's a scarab bracelet." Mam held up her find.

Bonnie plucked a circle pin from a nest of necklaces, the cheap chains of faded gilt tangled with some faux pearls. "I take it these are not the famous Bailey pearls."

"Oh, my goodness, no." Miss Augusta pursed her lips. "I don't know what Eliza was thinking, giving the Bailey pearls to that Porter girl Fort married. You would think when they divorced, she would have returned them to the family, but that's the Porters for you." She looked to Maudie, who tsked her affirmation. "That would have been the proper thing. Those pearls were quite valuable.

At least it wasn't the Comfort diamonds."

We all twitched, but Mam opened her mouth first. "Diamonds? Miss Eliza had diamonds? I never saw them."

Miss Augusta stared at Mam. "Well, you wouldn't have, would you? A lady doesn't wear diamonds during the day, except for her rings. Eliza stopped wearing hers because of her arthritis. I expect Fort has locked them in the bank vault, along with the others." She wafted her own bejeweled hand near her left ear. "The teardrops are quite fine, although perhaps not of the best quality. They've been in the Comfort family since before the war, and the brooch is supposed to be even older, and another piece older still."

"Eliza didn't wear any of them in recent times." Miss Maudie sighed. "What do you think, Augusta? Will Fort sell them, like everything else? He's the last of the Comforts, you know, and the Baileys who are left aren't close kin."

Miss Augusta's sniff indicated this was as it should be.

"Hey, look at these!" Mam, who had been sifting through the shoebox, held up a triple strand of red, white, and blue pop pearls.

Miss Augusta gave a small shudder. "Bicentennial beads! I can't imagine why anyone would keep those around."

Miss Maudie laughed. "Don't be such a snob, Augusta. I think I still have mine in a Whitman's Sampler box."

"Could I use them for the parade float?" Mam asked. "Maybe Cissy could wear them."

"I've decided we won't do a float this year," Miss Augusta said.

"Does that mean Pinckney won't be in the parade?" Mam was aggrieved. She shot me a look, as if I had somehow sabotaged her plans, but the float was a surprise to me, too.

"I didn't say that," Miss Augusta replied tartly. "Of course, Pinckney will be represented. I've offered the buggy to the chamber of commerce for Miss Palmetto, and Stephen is going on horseback as Lafayette. He'll have candy for the children in his saddlebag."

"Stephen?" Mam said.

"Candy?" Bonnie said.

"Lafayette?" I said.

"Yes, Stephen, our summer help. He's a Seabrook, y'know, so there's the Lafayette connection." Miss Augusta smiled with satisfaction. "And of course, Lafayette visited Pinckney and Indigo."

Even Mam was rendered speechless at Miss Augusta's revisionist version of local history. Yes, the French general had been hailed as a hero when he toured the South after the American Revolution. And he had bestowed his name on the baby daughter of William Seabrook while visiting the planter on Edisto Island. We all knew the story of Carolina Lafayette Seabrook of Cassina Point Plantation. But there were as many Seabrooks in the Low Country as shells on the beach, and plenty of boys were still christened Lafayette, although it was pronounced "Le-fate." But nowhere was there any indication that the Marquis de Lafayette had ever made a swing through Pinckney, handing out candy like it was Mardi Gras.

I looked to Miss Maudie to correct Miss Augusta, but she had nodded off again, and before Mam could pick up her jaw off the floor, Miss Augusta turned to her.

"Now, I'm counting on you, Margaret Ann, to find some suitable colonial garb in the costume closet with the tour-guide dresses. Boots, breeches, perhaps a wig. Lindsey, I'll need you to buy the candy. Wrapped peppermints, I think. If the grocery here doesn't have enough, you can run up to Centerville this afternoon after you greet the Aiken tour bus."

Miss Augusta had obviously forgotten I was off the rest of the day and tomorrow. I could probably pick up the candy on my way to Charleston, but the Aiken Garden Club wasn't on my agenda. Bonnie, bless her, came to my rescue.

"I'm meeting the bus," she said. "Remember, Lindsey's taking her holiday this weekend so she can be here on Monday."

Miss Augusta wasn't about to admit something had escaped her memory. "Ah, well, just make sure you have one of the best summer girls lead the Aiken tour. They'll have come from the

Charleston plantations, and we don't want Pinckney suffering by comparison. I'm spending a fortune keeping everything watered in this drought." She pushed her recliner back, a signal for us to leave.

As we gathered up our baubles and beads, Miss Augusta spoke again.

"Margaret Ann, since Lindsey is leaving us, you'll need to find Posey and make sure he's seen about getting the horse for Monday. And you best send young Stephen to me so I can apprise him of our plans."

We waited until we were outside before exploding into giggles.

"Lafayette!" Bonnie whooped.

"Can you believe—" Mam started sputtering.

"Shh," I admonished, dragging them up the path. "They'll hear us!"

"What?" Bonnie pretended to play with a hearing aid. "What did you say? Speak up." She collapsed into another giggle fit.

Mam was fuming. "At least your charms don't look like Miss Maudie!"

"But I'm like Miss Maudie," Bonnie asserted, holding up her teapot so the faceted crystal caught the sunlight. "I like something a little sparkly. I'm going to wear the durn thing so everyone can see it. I'll just be Miss Too-Tacky-for-Words."

"At least you won't be in the parade," I said, grinning. "Mam, you need to find 'young Stephen' and tell him to go see Miss Augusta. I wish I could be a fly on the wall when he finds out his Le-fate!"

CHAPTER ELEVEN

Romancing the Sheriff

As fate would have it, the drawbridge was open so a yacht the size of a mini cruise ship could meander its way down the Intracoastal. To heck with all us po' folks lined up on either side having to turn off our engines and roll down windows, lest we spontaneously combust in the July sun. So much for my girly primping, which had held up while I threw my overnight bag in the front seat and dropped off Doc at Mam's. I was going to melt if that big boat didn't get a move on.

At last! I hit the high button on the A.C. as the traffic snailed its way across the old bridge. Even more cars were coming onto the island, mostly SUVs loaded down with bikes and surfboards, towing Jet Skis or boats. Really, Indigo needed either a gate or a new bridge. As a native, I wanted the gate—who were all these people on my island?—but I also knew a bridge was as inevitable as the tide of tourists flowing in for the holiday.

Traffic thinned out on the River Road leading to the highway and Charleston. I was almost to the Granville County line when I heard a siren despite my oldies radio station and saw the blue flashing light on my tail.

Hey, I wasn't speeding, I thought as I slowed and eased to

where the grassy shoulder widened. Maybe this was Olivia playing a joke on me, although she was all business on the job. But maybe there was some message from Will, or about Will. My stomach tightened.

It wasn't Olivia. The young deputy walking toward me was one I didn't recognize, perhaps a recent recruit, judging by the peach fuzz on his dimpled chin. What a cutie! I turned down the Beach Boys singing about their California girls.

"Hello, officer," I said, the humid air invading my cool cocoon. I smiled innocently—well, I was innocent, wasn't I?—and pushed my sunglasses on top of my forehead.

"License and registration, ma'am," he said seriously, and then looked intently at the items I handed over. "Um, ma'am," he said. "You have a North Carolina driver's license and license plate. But don't you live on Indigo? I mean, aren't you Major McLeod's uh, uh . . ."

"Friend," I said firmly. "I used to live in Charlotte, but I'm staying with my parents on Indigo at the moment."

"Aren't you out at Pinckney?"

"I'm working there some, if that's what you mean, but I don't live there."

"Oh, sorry, my mistake. I thought that you and the major were . . ." He stumbled, his ears turning red. He recovered quickly, though. "It's just that if you're planning on staying on the island, you need to get a South Carolina license and registration. That is, if you're staying?"

Good question. I started to explain that I was between houses, but kindergarten cop didn't really need to know my complicated living situation, so I smiled again. "I'll keep that in mind. Thanks for bringing it to my attention"—I squinted at his nameplate— "Officer Walters. I hope you have a good holiday."

"You, too, Miss Fox. Drive safe, now."

I let out a sigh as he headed back to his cruiser and I rolled up the window. Was I ever going to see my deputy? And would my bangs be dry by then?

❀

A blast of wonderfully cold air hit me as I pushed through the double glass doors of the posh hotel. My smart little black sling-backs tapped on the marble floor as I quickly walked past the reception desk. Will had left me a voice mail earlier to say he would meet me in the lobby around three. I scanned the vast seating area as I circled the double curving staircase. The elegant chandelier loomed overhead, discreetly diffusing its light through tiers of brilliants. As my eyes traveled back down, they found a pair of smoky blue eyes that were looking me up and down like I was a Godiva chocolate just waiting to be gobbled up. I walked over to the man who had occupied my thoughts daily the last six months.

"Welcome back to the Low Country, Will." My voice was amazingly calm, though I sure wasn't.

He didn't say a word but gently ran his finger along my jaw line and pulled me close. Hugging me, he murmured into my hair, "You look beautiful, Lindsey. I've missed you."

Oh, my. This was going way better than I had hoped. Obviously, the short skirt and sleeveless, low-cut top were having the desired effect. I backed up to give him the once-over and noticed that he also had dressed to impress. The blue polo matching his eyes looked as if the tags had been removed only moments before.

"You don't look so bad yourself." I suddenly felt shy. Talking on the phone a few nights a week didn't make up for the physical separation. Will and I had just been getting used to being a couple when a special assignment had sent him out of state. I was pretty sure from the veiled hints—"I'm losing my summer tan"—that he was in the mountains of northern Georgia or western North Carolina, both backwoods havens for meth labs.

Now that I was standing next to him, I could tell he wasn't as coppery brown as usual, but he still looked good, mighty good. We kept gazing at each other as if to say, "Now what?" Then Will broke the spell by taking my hand and leading me down the shop-lined mall. "How about afternoon tea in the restaurant over there?"

Bless his heart. He was trying so hard to please. I smiled. "I don't think so. You won't believe it, but I just saw Aunt Cora going in with some of the church ladies. Don't worry, she didn't see us, but let's go this way." I pulled him out a side door. "How about something cold? And a little more private?"

He grinned that wonderful grin I had missed so much. "Sounds like my cup of tea."

Five minutes later, waffle cones dripping in our hands, we strolled down Market Street gazing in shop windows. Privacy was in short supply, and the heat was waging war on my Fudge Brownies and Cream cone, but I didn't mind. I was licking the overflow on my fingers while Will, who had demolished his Butter Pecan in three bites, began playing catch-up, questioning me about my parents and pets.

Then came the inevitable: "So, how are the cousins?"

"Oh, y'know, just like themselves." I took a big gulp of ice cream and then had to press my hand against my neck as the cold eased down. "Maybe more so, with the holiday coming up." I cleared my throat.

"Want to tell me how you got that bruise on your forehead?" he asked softly.

Oh, great. My makeup had melted as fast as the ice cream. "Trying to get a cutting of a rosebush for Margaret Ann. I swear, she gets bossier by the day. I just slipped and banged myself a little on a limb." I silently congratulated myself on being evasive. We had communicated mostly by voice mail this week, so I was hoping he only knew the broad outline of recent events—the bridge going out, the brouhaha surrounding Miss Eliza's funeral, the fire at Comfort's End—and not our interactive roles.

"Would that limb be attached to a tree near the cemetery?"

Rats. I wondered who had ratted us out. "Mmm, possibly." I finished my cone and dropped the sticky napkin in a handy waste can.

I really didn't want to waste our wonderful getaway bickering about what Will regarded as our meddling. God must have taken pity on me because just then a loud clap of thunder sounded. As Nanny would say, "The bottom just fell out!" Will grabbed my hand, and we sprinted across Meeting Street through the frog-strangling downpour.

"I wish we could get some of this rain on Indigo," I said, shaking off the drops. Wet hair again. "It's still really dry. But I'm sure not. How far to your friend Chuck's place? Isn't that where we're staying?"

Will grinned mischievously. "Right up the elevator."

"Oh, duh." Chuck's place. Charleston Place. How had I let that one get by me? Will was loving his surprise.

"I'll go get your stuff from your car," he said. "Swap you a room key for a car key?"

"Deal."

"The pleasure is mine."

And mine, I thought as I dodged two ladies in matching straw hats and walked over to the alcove with two banks of elevators. I yawned. My thoughts were of taking off my cute but uncomfortable little shoes. Then maybe a nap before dinner. Then again, maybe not. The elevator dinged. Such a universal sound, that ding. It would really throw people if it chimed out a tune like our cell phones. I must be tired if my mind was wandering to such nonsense.

⚬

Waking to the sound of Will's voice talking softly on the phone in the suite's other room, I snuggled deeper into the ebony four-poster bed. The clock on the table winked in the dimness. Seven o'clock! My nap had lasted two hours. The bedroom door opened a crack.

"Time for happy hour," Will whispered, walking to the bed with two wineglasses. Easing down, he leaned over and gave me a Chardonnay kiss. "We've reservations downstairs at the grill in forty-five minutes."

"I could get used to happy hours like this." I sipped the wine.

"If you play your cards right, I just might do this . . . on a real regular basis." He gave me a direct look, and I proceeded to choke on my Chardonnay.

"Sorry," I hiccupped. "First time drinking wine at Chuck's place." I leaned back against the downy pillows. "Um, who were you talking to just now?"

"Just work stuff." Now who was being evasive?

"I'm sure not checking in with Miss Augusta. As for Bonnie and Mam, they're going to get voice mail on my cell phone. I turned it off as soon as I parked." I chattered on while Will just kept looking at me, a small smile on his lips. "Besides, they're busy with their kids, although Bonnie has her sister worried about how much time she's spending with Wayne Jenkins. I think I told you he took her and the boys crabbing. We think Bonnie is craving male attention, since Tom has been gone so long." I paused for a sip.

"Do you ever crave male attention, Lindsey?" Will's eyes twinkled.

"Only a certain male's," I quipped. Who was this flirty female who had taken over my body? "Only now you need to scram for a few minutes so I can get ready for dinner. I'm going to take advantage of that gorgeous marble bathroom. You outdid yourself, sport. This is really a beautiful place to stay."

"Wait, what's this? Where's my gator?" His finger touched the teapot charm and then grazed my throat.

"It's a reproduction silver teapot," I said. "Miss Augusta gave us each one. They were in a box from the estate sale. I better take it off."

"Here, I'll help."

❧

The next morning, I was wrapped in a fluffy bathrobe flipping through a hotel magazine while Will devoured the breakfast he had ordered up to our suite. I couldn't eat a thing after all the shrimp and grits I had put away the night before. Oh, well, maybe a biscuit to go with my morning Coke. Will had remembered I wasn't a coffee girl. As I reached for the strawberry jam, he looked up from the sports section of the *Post and Courier* and grinned.

"You want a biscuit to go with that jam?"

"Yup," I said. "Did you know that Charleston Place is owned by the same company that owns the Orient Express? The last time I was in London, I splurged on one of their day trips to Leeds Castle. Now, I want to go to Scotland on the train."

"Count me in," Will said. "Land of my ancestors. And maybe you could show me around London first. I warn you, I want to play tourist and see the changing of the guard at Buckingham Palace and go to the Tower of London."

"Fine with me. The Crown Jewels are gorgeous. You wouldn't believe the size of those emeralds and rubies, and all the diamonds. You can hardly believe they're real, they're so big."

"Maybe they're not," Will said. "Maybe they're glass, and the real ones are locked in a dungeon."

"They're sort of in a dungeon, but they're not fakes. Glass and paste don't sparkle like the real thing."

"I didn't know you were so into diamonds." Will set down his coffee cup. "Maybe we need to explore this subject more in depth."

I had a mouthful of biscuit, so I was saved from saying anything. How had we moved so fast from Charleston to London, the Crown Jewels, and diamonds? Talk about your Orient Express.

Will's cell phone gave off a businesslike ring from a side table. Saved by the bell!—what a cliché. While he answered it, I decided to go check mine for messages. Maybe Mam was having a problem with Lafayette's costume. I smiled at the idea; I'd have to tell Will. But my smile vanished when I heard R. W.'s voice mail.

Then I began packing.

April 30

I stayed up late last night to finish Rebecca, *by Daphne du Maurier. J. lent it to me. She said I would like it. I loved it! It is so romantic. At first, I thought the narrator was named Rebecca like me, but she is really the hero's beautiful first wife who died. The narrator—she doesn't have a name, which is strange—is the new wife, and she thinks she should be more like Rebecca. There's this creepy housekeeper who shows her all around Manderley, the big house on Cornwall. Rebecca's room is just like she left it. The housekeeper asks her if she believes in ghosts, if she thinks the dead watch the living. Very spooky. J. says Alfred Hitchcock made a movie out of the book a long time ago. Maybe it will be on TV sometime and Grandmother will let me watch it. She thinks she is so strict and that is why I make good grades. She doesn't know I sneak out so I can meet R. at the graveyard. She doesn't hear anything, ever.*

CHAPTER TWELVE
Swamp Fox, Meet Cinderella

Cars and trucks were packed like sardines on the dirt field that once had been a miniature-golf course before its owner sold out to a condo developer who was still waiting on zoning variances. Personally, I couldn't imagine living where the only view was the parking lot of the Pig, which today was serving as the staging area for the island's Fourth of July parade. It was set to start at nine in the morning, the idea being that there'd still be plenty of time for other holiday activities and it might not be as hot. Fat chance. At quarter of nine, the tide was dead low, so there was no breeze off the beach, and the sun was beating down on the asphalt.

I found Mam adding palms, red and white carnations, and lots of red, white, and blue ribbons to the Pinckney buggy. The infamous bicentennial beads adorned the black horse's braided mane and tail. Stephen Seabrook was standing near another horse, a rangy bay. But why was he wearing a coonskin cap? Where was Lafayette?

"We're going with Swamp Fox instead," said Mam before I could open my mouth. "We couldn't find a wig that didn't look like Marie Antoinette. You know, 'Swamp Fox, Swamp Fox, tail on his hat.' Francis Marion was a Revolutionary War patriot, too."

"Who didn't come anywhere near Indigo either," I noted. There was a reason the Francis Marion Forest was north of Charleston. "Here are the peppermints."

I'd had plenty of time to pick them up yesterday afternoon after my weekend getaway had been cut short. I'd been pretty short with Will, too.

"Exactly when were you planning on telling me that this was a one-night stand and that you're coming back to Indigo to take over the investigations?" I'd asked as I stuffed hotel toiletries into my cosmetic case. After all, we wouldn't be needing those nice little soaps.

"How do you know?" Will leaned against the door, arms folded. "I just got the call confirming the reassignment."

"But you knew it was coming last night." I tightened the cap on a tiny shampoo bottle before adding it to my stash. Will's coming home put me in an ethical dilemma regarding Becky's notebook. I hadn't even had time to read the durned thing. Maybe there wouldn't be anything relevant in it.

"I didn't want to spoil our time alone," Will said. "Besides, I thought you'd be happy to have me on Indigo again."

"I am." I zipped the case shut. No need to let him know the cousins were playing Nancy Drew. He'd find out soon enough. I smiled brightly. "I'm just disappointed I'll have to share you with work and we won't have the rest of today and tonight." And that you didn't tell me. "By the way, R. W. said he'd like to talk with you before this afternoon's press conference."

Will's jaw tightened. "I thought you weren't writing news anymore."

"I'm not," I said. "R. W. just thought I might know how to get hold of you."

Mam brought me back to the present. "You hold onto the peppermints, or give them to Stephen. Where is Miss Palmetto?"

"Coming this way."

No way you could miss Zora Manigault, one of Marietta's many grand-nieces. In her royal blue prom gown, her tiara sparkling in the sun and her title sash stretched across her ample bust, the tall teenager sailed across the parking lot like the *Queen Mary*.

"You look very majestic," Mam said. "Let me pin this corsage on your shoulder, and then you can get in the buggy. You sure you don't want someone to drive you?"

"No, ma'am." Zora's teeth were almost as bright as the tiara. She patted the horse affectionately. "Me and Blackjack here are old pals. Did Aunt Marietta tell you I'm going to be a horse vet? I think that's how come I got to be Miss Palmetto. Y'know, it's not just looks. I do volunteer work at the equine center."

I wondered how the parade queen was going to wave to her subjects, but Zora jumped in the buggy and took the reins in one capable white-gloved hand. Alrighty. Stephen had mounted up as well, and I stuffed peppermints in his saddlebag. Time to get this parade on the road.

Mam saw them off. "Posey will meet you at the end with the horse trailers at the Baptist church." She turned to me. "Come on. Let's cross before the band."

I trotted after her, noticing the tuba player was already red in the face. It was unbearably humid. I should have given Zora a Jesus fan. "Is there any shade?"

"Sort of." Mam pointed to the BP gas station, where Bonnie had set up lawn chairs at an umbrella table. Ben and Sam were standing right in front at the curb with Chad Henderson, a redhead between two towheads. Behind us, the band started in on "Yankee Doodle Dandy," and everybody cheered. A color guard marched first, followed by veterans in decorated golf carts. Wayne Jenkins waved at us—or maybe just at Bonnie, who was blushing.

"I didn't know he was a war hero until Miss Augusta mentioned it last night," she said.

Mam and I exchanged glances as Bonnie waved at the golf-cart brigade. Then Mam whooped. "Oh, look. The girls are next!"

Here came her exercise class, Faithfully Fit Forever, which met twice a week at the Baptist church. Mam would have been right in there marching if she hadn't been overseeing the Pinckney crew, so she hollered and whistled as her pals stepped and kicked their way down the street. They did look pretty fit in their white shorts and hot-pink Ts, although Sally Simmons's shorts strained across her rump. Maybe she liked them tight.

"Sally is a new member," said Mam, uncannily reading my thoughts not for the first time. "But they look good, don't they?"

"God helps those that help themselves," muttered Bonnie.

"Hush!" Mam was defensive. "I don't see y'all exercising. You don't burn many calories crabbing, y'know. It's not like throwing a shrimp net."

"That's not exercise," I said. "That's work."

"So is Faithfully Fit, which you'd know if you ever got up early enough to come with me." Mam tripped over her purse handle and sat down with a thump.

"Watch out, Margaret Ann," I said as I caught some of the objects rolling out. "Why do you have a bottle of Cosequin in your purse? Isn't that for dogs?"

"Yeah, it's Chloe's," Mam said. "For her joints."

"But why is it in your purse?"

"Long story short, I took it accidentally this morning."

Bonnie laughed. "Oh, instead of your own."

"No, I took my joint stuff, too. I mixed it up with my calcium, which I didn't take. I knew right away the pill was too large as it lumped down my throat. I tried to gag it up, but no luck."

"Mam, you should have called the vet or the doctor or somebody." Bonnie looked concerned.

"That's why the bottle's in my purse," Mam replied. "I called both of them on my cell on my way here. The vet said to call Dr. Papodopolus. His nurse called back and said I was fine as long as I wasn't scratching behind my ears."

"And are you?" There are times when I cannot believe my cousin.

"Of course not!" Mam was indignant. "You two can stop laughing now. The nurse said she's done it before. Look, there's the Gatortorium float."

Ben, Chad, and Sam were jumping up and down on the curb

at the sight of a gator-costumed character and a trainer wearing a large snake around his neck. Mam flinched. "Too much nature."

Next was the Lions Club flatbed advertising bingo and playing Sousa marches on a loudspeaker. Daddy would have helped if he were here. He loves Sousa. I hoped he got to hear some on the ship.

Then came Olivia in her sheriff's car. Mam turned to me. "Have you seen Will since he got back?"

"No." I'd told her what had happened—well, not all of it—when I picked up Doc early. "But I did shove a copy of Becky's notebook in a manila envelope in the station's drop box this morning before anyone was there. Have you read it yet?" I lowered my voice. "There's some odd stuff in there. We need to talk."

"I know." Mam's brow furrowed. "Bonnie and I think so, too. Becky sure didn't like Fort."

"Speak of the devil." Bonnie nodded toward the other side of the street, where parade viewers were three and four deep in front of the pavilion. The sun flashed off her teapot charm, which she was wearing diamond side out defiantly. I had slipped mine on the chain next to my gator charm. Looking over, I saw Mam's chubby teapot bobbing on her white shirt.

"I see him," she said. "Maybe my dark glasses are scratchy, but he looks like he's glaring at us!"

The Piggly Wiggly float momentarily blocked my view, but as it rounded the corner, I saw Fort. "You're right, I think. Who wears mirrored shades these days, for Pete's sake?"

"He really gives me the creeps," said Mam, "Sort of like Rabbit, only different, if you know what I mean."

I did. We fell silent as two fire trucks with flashing lights followed the Pig float. Ben was pushing his arm up and down in the air in hopes of hearing a siren, but I knew it wouldn't sound till the end of the parade.

"He's not there anymore," Bonnie said as the fire truck moved on. "I don't know where he's gone, but I'm happy he's not looking this way." She called to Ben, Chad, and Sam, "Boys, stay on the curb. And look! It's Cinderella. How cuuute. Aw!"

Chad crowed, "That's not Cinderella! It's a goat!"

"Her name is Cinderella." I smiled at the unofficial town goat, who lived in the field behind town hall some of the time. She was housebroken, so everyone said, and when she was home, she stayed in. One of these days, I was going to get around to freelancing a feature on her to my former employer, *Perfect Pet* magazine. Now, she was decked out in a straw hat, pulling her goat cart full of phone books and cans. The sign on her cart was cute, too: "Remember to Recycle."

"Why is that funny?" Ben asked me as he reached to get a drink box off the table.

"Well, Ben, when her owners leave the house, they always give her a phone book to chew, so she won't chew up the furniture or anything else."

"Yeah, she is her own recycling center," Mam added. "Or more like a shredder!"

"Here, Ben, take drinks to the others," said Bonnie, looking puzzled. "Oh, I get it now." She grinned, shaking her hair. "Remember, I'm a blonde. Do you know what you call a blonde who picks up the newspaper in the driveway?"

"A golden retriever." Honestly. "Hey, I've got one for you. Two blondes are on a mountain in Tennessee looking at the moon, and one asks the other, 'Which do you think is farther, the moon or Disney World?' And the other says, 'Duh. Disney World. You can see the moon from here.'"

"Ha-ha." Bonnie flipped her hair again, flicking her chain in the process. The teapot charm went flying.

I picked it up from the brownish grass. "You need to fix the clasp on this. Put it in your pocket for now. Miss Augusta will have a hissy fit if you lose it."

"Need any help, ladies?"

Fort's deep voice startled us. He and his antiques pal, Gibbs Henry, had moved to our side of the street and come up from behind. Fort had removed his sunglasses to reveal bleary eyes.

Angry red blood vessels threaded across his nose. Gauze bandaged the back of his left hand. I smelled gin.

"Oh, Fort, how are you?" Mam asked. Suddenly, she was feeling sorry for the old goat. "We are so sorry about the fire and Rabbit and everything. Such a shame, your mama's things . . ." She was starting to babble.

Fort bowed his head. "A shame, yes." He looked intently at us, then strode off back toward the gas station, Gibbs on his heels like a loyal terrier.

"Uh, goodbye," Mam said. "Bonnie Lynn, let go of my arm!"

"That was strange," said Bonnie, dropping Mam's elbow. "Sorry, Mam, I was afraid you would mention Becky or the diary."

"I know better than that!" Mam retorted. "I wonder where he and Gibbs are going. He's a shady character, too. Did you see that palmetto hat?"

"Panama hat," Bonnie said. "Pa-na-ma."

"I know. Whatever." Mam turned back toward the parade. A small drum-and-fife corps marched past us, playing something vaguely patriotic. "There's Miss Palmetto!"

Zora gave a beauty-queen wave with a pleated fan. Smart girl!

"And don't forget Swamp Fox!" Bonnie pointed at Stephen, who threw peppermints at the boys. They scrambled for the candy. "Stay here on the grass!"

Ben leaped up, peppermints in hand. "Mama, that's my Davy Crockett hat!"

Chapter Thirteen
Fireworks All Around

Mam dropped a straw beach hat on my desk at Pinckney. "This is yours."

"What are you doing with it?"

"You forgot it after we went crabbing. I put it in the backseat of the Tahoe, and I was going to give it to you at the parade, but then Cinderella needed it. She ate hers."

"Ah." That would explain the faint farm-animal aroma emanating from what had been my favorite sun hat. Oh, well. "Where's Bonnie?"

"Dropping the boys off with the Hendersons and Chad for the afternoon." Mam sat in the chair and pulled Becky's notebook from her tote bag. "She said to start without her. I think she's on drugs."

I knew she meant Becky, not Bonnie. "Because she was smoking in the cemetery? That could be cigarettes and not dope."

Mam frowned. "She sounds sort of dopey, though, all dreamy about R., whoever he is."

"She's a teenager, for heaven's sake. She's either in love or thinks she is. And she can't wait to get away from Indigo. She wants to leave when J. does. J. is her best friend." I thumbed through my copy of the notebook. "It's an unequal friendship, though. Becky wants to be like J. She tries to dress like her, and she reads what

J. reads and adopts her opinions. There's that place where she's writing about the Vietnam War and how she thinks it's so cool that J. has been to a peace demonstration. And y'know that wasn't on Indigo. The sixties didn't really get here till the seventies."

Mam nodded. "I know, because there's that part about Fort wanting to enlist like all his Citadel buddies, only he's got some heart murmur. He hates that he can't go, especially because his older brother got killed in Korea and is a big hero to Miss Eliza. The way Becky tells it, he drinks way too much. It's why his first wife left him and he's moved back to Comfort's End, where his mama waits on him hand and foot, even though he's not a hero."

"J. doesn't like him, though, Becky says. She can't stand being anywhere near him. And then Becky writes, 'If she only knew, but I can't tell her.' That sounds—"

"—like Becky knows something bad about Fort," Mam interrupted.

"More than just that he's on his way to being an alcoholic, though, because apparently everybody and his brother knows that, just like now. Some sort of secret . . ."

"The KKK!" Mam asserted. "He could have been in the Klan. Remember, there were still posters on telephone poles about meetings when we were coming along. And didn't a black family on the island get burned out in the sixties?"

"I don't know about that. House fires happen. But again, everyone seemed to know that blacks weren't welcome at Comfort's End."

"Maybe Fort was seeing a black girl and got her in trouble. Think of the scandal if that got out."

"So he's in the Klan and has a black girlfriend? I don't think it worked like that. This was the 1960s, not the 1860s. But Fort could have been tomcatting around. Somebody who was married, or lots younger."

"Maybe Fort hit on J.," Mam ventured.

"Or he hit on Becky. Maybe more."

"Oh, gross!" Mam shuddered. "He's her uncle, even if he's not that much older. I hate to think about it."

"I know. Me, too. But it could make sense." The more I read Becky's notebook, the more troubled I became. What appeared to be adolescent emoting over her appearance and her crush on R. was shadowed by a true unhappiness about life at Comfort's End. Maybe I was reading between the lines, but all wasn't right in that family. "Think about it," I told Mam. "It might explain why she hates Fort and dislikes her grandmother. And it's such a huge thing that she can't tell her best friend, or even write about it. That's not uncommon with sexual-abuse victims. They separate themselves from it, go into denial."

"Like the guests on *Oprah*." Mam was talking faster now. "They're ashamed, they think it's their fault, especially if it's a family friend or a stepfather or, ugh, an uncle. They feel powerless. People didn't talk about abuse back then. It wasn't all over talk shows with celebrities. It was a dark family secret." Mam's eyes widened. "Do you think Fort killed Becky? He would have had a motive if she threatened to tell someone, although I bet Miss Eliza wouldn't have believed her precious son could do that."

"But J. would have, if Becky finally did tell her." I stopped. Something I was trying to remember, something that kept slipping away . . . "And J. was somebody Miss Eliza would believe because—"

"—because J. is Julia." Bonnie stood in the doorway. "It's obvious."

❧

It was obvious I wasn't going to find a parking place anywhere near the river pier. Actually, the pier was the end, or beginning, of an old bridge before the new drawbridge, which was no longer new. This pier, with benches added along the side, was a great place to crab or fish or watch fireworks on the Fourth. Fireworks were banned from the beach, so the island sponsored a "controlled" display from a barge on the river. Some communities had canceled fireworks this year because of the drought, but the river barge had been judged safe, as long as there wasn't any wind. And there wasn't. Indigo continued to bake even as the sun sank like a molten stone on the horizon.

I hiked in from the north forty, passing people of all ages sitting in the backs of trucks or in folding lawn chairs. It was like a giant tailgate party, as if the crowd from the parade had coalesced at the pier on the other side of the island. There even was a refreshment stand. I smelled popcorn. Soon, it would be dark enough for the fireworks to begin. Bonnie had talked me into coming, wanting me to see the fireworks with the boys for the first time. Now, she was nowhere to be found. But maybe I'd see someone from Becky's generation who could confirm our suspicions about the diary, although Bonnie the lawyer had made a good case for J. as Julia. She was right—it was obvious, once you picked up on the clues. But we still didn't know R.'s identity.

Bonnie suddenly emerged from the refreshment line. "Hey, we're over at the picnic tables with the Hendersons so the boys can see. The pier looks too crowded." She handed me a tub of popcorn. "Carry this over to them. Wayne bought some sparklers and poppers for them to play with."

"Where are you going?"

"Back in line. They've got Fried Twinkies. You want one?"

"No thanks." My taste for sweets only went so far. "But get me a Diet Coke." I reached in my pocket for some change, but she waved me off.

As I headed over to the picnic area, I saw Cissy on the pier flipping her hair while she talked to Stephen Seabrook. No doubt, Mama and Aunt Boodie would figure out which ocean this Seabrook hailed from as soon as they returned end of the week. And Will wondered why we cousins were such snoops. Obviously, it was in our genes.

I spotted Wayne and Mam waving sparklers with Bonnie's boys and Chad. Whoa, there was Fort not too far away, his white shirt standing out in the deepening twilight, a cigarette glowing in his right hand. Had he always smoked? And was he watching our little gathering? Or was he just waiting on the fireworks? If so, why was he underneath that live oak? The view wouldn't be very good.

Kathy Henderson made room on the bench beside her. She and her husband played golf all the time, it seemed, or else they were riding bikes. Way too athletic for me. Still, she didn't look old enough to have a grandson the same age as Ben, but I knew she was in her fifties. Wait a minute . . .

"Hey Kathy," I said. "Did you know Becky Bailey when you were in high school?"

"Oh, sure. She was ahead of me a couple years, but the school wasn't that big. We didn't hang out, though. She was kind of arty, I remember." Kathy shook her head. "Isn't it just awful, them finding her bones like that after all these years?" She lowered her voice confidingly. "Margaret Ann said y'all were there."

Aha! Of course Mam couldn't keep her trap shut. "Mmm," I assented.

Kathy's hazel eyes widened. "Oh, I would have just up and died if that was me! Personally, I'm thinking of being cremated if I can convince Chub. He wants to go to Orangeburg with his people, but I think you have to be a member at Trinity there now or they won't let you in."

I tried to look sympathetic. This was not the direction I wanted to steer the conversation. "I'm doing some background stuff for R. W. at the paper. Do you remember who Becky hung around with back then?"

"R. W. doesn't remember?" Kathy's eyebrows shot up. "Goodness, he was part of that same group that put out the yearbook and the newspaper."

I quickly backtracked. "Uh, I think maybe he meant Becky's friends on Indigo. Y'know, island people, maybe somebody she rode to school with, or dated."

"Oh." Kathy was satisfied. "I don't know who she went out with. Ron and Ray Simmons had a car, and I think she might have ridden to school with them till they graduated. Fort probably took her some, too. You could ask him. I think I saw him here."

"No, that's okay," I put in hurriedly. "I'll catch up with him later."

Boom! I jumped as the first rockets went off, spilling some popcorn on the ground. I looked up to see a burst of blues and purples. Pretty. But my favorites were the white-and-gold fountains that filled the sky as they slowly spilled to the water. Wait, where was Fort going with Wayne? They had moved away from the crowd and appeared to be arguing about something.

"Wayne left already?" I asked Mam, who had returned to the bench, scrunching in between me and Kathy.

"No, he'll be back in a minute. Fort needed to talk to him." She took the popcorn.

"What about?" My words were lost as more rockets whistled overhead and exploded.

"Something about—" The booms drowned Mam out. Amazing. She tried again. "Dental records."

Bonnie appeared, handing me a cold can. The boys had clambered on top of the table. Smoke was in the air, a haze over the barge.

Boom! I jumped again. I couldn't help it even when I knew it was coming.

"Cool," said Ben.

"Way cool," said Mam, trying to sound like Cissy.

"Awesome." Another voice came out of the darkness.

"Huh?" said Mam and Bonnie together, turning at the same time.

I spun around and almost fell. "Will! You startled us!" I jumped again as the next rocket went off.

"You sure it's me?" He put his hand on my shoulder. "You seem kind of nervous."

That didn't really describe it. Fireworks above, Will beside me. I felt all tingly, combustible.

"Hey, Will." Mam clutched at Ben's arm in the lull. "Ben, Sam, Chad—y'all come meet Sheriff Will. He's a good friend of the family." Her elbow poked me in the ribs.

Will shook their hands. "Nice to meet you, boys," he said. Will had a way of making everyone feel important.

"Are you really a sheriff?" Ben asked. "You don't look like one."

"That's because I'm not wearing my uniform. Y'all enjoy the fireworks while I borrow your aunt for a minute."

"Where are we going?" I asked. Will might be wearing faded jeans, but he didn't seem off duty. I thought we'd smoothed things over at the hotel yesterday—quite satisfactorily, in my opinion. But now . . .

"This way." His hand, firmly placed on the small of my back, guided me toward his truck. "Here." He opened my door.

"Why, Will, are we parking?" I tried to keep the tone light. It didn't work. He shut my door and walked purposefully to the other side of the truck, not saying anything as he turned the ignition, rolled up the windows, and turned on the air.

"Start from the beginning, Lindsey Fox."

Wow, Fox. He really was serious, mad even.

"The beginning?" I asked softly in my most innocent voice. "You already know we just happened to be in the graveyard last week."

"And that you spilled details to R. W. for the paper, Miss Unidentified Source."

Oh, good. He didn't know I'd actually written the story. "Like I said, we just happened on the scene."

"And I suppose you just happened to discover the diary of the presumed victim? A copy of which just happened to show up in my office this morning?"

I should have known this was coming. "Yes, we did just happen to find it, or rather Mam did, after the estate sale, in this bench she bought."

"And you didn't think this might be important evidence that the authorities needed right away?"

"We didn't even know what it was until after we read it, and that wasn't until after Mam left it in the boat at Rabbit's fish camp."

"Fish camp!" Will slammed his fist on the dash. "When were you there, and who said it was Rabbit's?"

"Rabbit said it was, before he told us to get out. And don't get mad with me! We didn't know he was there when we went back."

"Back? You were there before?"

"On Thursday night when the boat got stuck on that side of the bridge because of the tide, only don't tell J. T. because he doesn't know."

This time, the thunderous boom of more fireworks stopped me. We were missing the finale. But Will looked like he might explode. He was fighting to control his anger. And now I was mad, too. Why did Will always assume the worst where the cousins were concerned? If I heard his lecture one more time about amateur sleuths thinking murder was some sort of game . . . Didn't he realize by now that we didn't plan on getting involved in crime fighting? Not really, anyway.

Will was hunched over the steering wheel, his shoulders quivering. Omigosh! Was he having some kind of fit? Wait, was he laughing?

He was. "You really can't help it, can you? Of all women, I have to fall for one who keeps falling over dead bodies. Oh, geez, Lindsey, what am I going to do with you?"

He didn't wait for an answer. His kiss left me breathless.

He leaned back against his seat and said something under his breath. "Okay, seriously, I need to know what you and the cousins know or think you know. From the beginning."

"Okay." I took in a breath. Here goes . . .

"Is that all?" Will asked when I finished with our suspicions about Fort.

"I think so." I hadn't told him that we thought J. was Julia. She was dead and gone anyway, and Miss Augusta had enough bad memories to contend with. I also hadn't said anything about the Comfort curse. Marietta wouldn't appreciate being dragged into something that was just superstition, obviously. But Fort, Rabbit, the fish camp, the fire—those were facts, on the record, as was Becky's dislike of her uncle.

"And you didn't tell me any of this Saturday night when we were together?"

"We didn't know some of it. Besides . . ." Why did I feel so flushed? I'm way too young for hot flashes. I looked for something to cool myself down. What was that on the floorboard, a church bulletin? I grabbed it and started fanning.

"Besides?" Will was grinning.

"Besides, if you remember correctly, I was a bit preoccupied. You were distracting me." I kept fanning.

"I was, wasn't I?" His voice was soft as he reached for me.

Obviously, the fireworks weren't over after all. Obviously.

May 8

The yearbooks are here. They look really good, if I say so myself. We have started writing in them. I am saving space for J. and R. at the back. They will have to be careful what they write because I'm sure Grandmother will try and read it. W. wrote that he hopes I have a good summer and he hopes to see me! I didn't know he even knew I existed. He is so cool. We graduate in one month. Finally. I am sick of this place. J. is talking about leaving in June, but maybe she will wait. R. has a job at the landing, so I will be able to see him without anyone knowing anything. I think somebody else was in the graveyard the other night, but R. didn't hear anything. He threw a beer can in the woods where I thought there was something, and nothing happened. Who said, "The night has a thousand eyes"? Grandmother saw the bruise on my arm. I told her I got it playing volleyball in gym.

CHAPTER FOURTEEN
Someone's Been Here

"Hurry, these things are eating me alive!" I yelled as I rushed from the CR-V to the closest door of Mam's house.

Obviously, the whimsical sign posted on a pine in the drive said it all: "Danger, Mosquitoes!" No one knew better than I. The immunity I'd enjoyed as an island girl had deserted me over the years. One bite now would be an itchy welt within minutes. I didn't have enough salt water in my veins to ward off an attack.

I ran past the drop cloths and sawhorses and down the oyster-shell path that used to lead to the back door but now ended sooner at the new sunroom door. Thank goodness Mam had left the outside lights on. Otherwise, I might have broken my neck, she had so many iron borders and what she called "yard art." Missing those but tripping up the steps, I yanked at the new screen door. Cissy had pulled up her Civic beside me and scooted in on my heels as Mam and Bonnie parked in the front. The ever-helpful Hendersons had taken the boys home for ice cream, so time for another chick night—chocolate, wine, and more diary discussion.

"Your new door sticks," I called to Mam in the front foyer.

"What?" She sounded exasperated.

I looked around her new porch. The terra-cotta tile floor was perfect.

"Oh, man, the door shut." Mam was definitely put out.

"So?" said Cissy, perched on the new vanity stool with her newly acquired seventeen-year-old attitude.

"So," said Mam, giving her "the look," à la Miss Augusta. "I left it propped open with that thing," she said, pointing to a frog planter I had given her for her birthday. Actually, I had regifted. I should be ashamed, but I don't have a green thumb, and she did like it. Now, it had fallen on its side into the flower bed. "I promised Meatball I would let the paint dry overnight. Now it's messed up, and he's going to have to paint the door again! Could it have blown shut with the planter holding it open? No way. It wouldn't have blown down the steps. No, it couldn't have, it's not even windy." Mam often answered her own questions.

"I just love that name," said Bonnie, avoiding the paint and repropping the frog planter against the door.

"What? Oh, you mean, Meatball?" asked Mam.

"Yeah, I keep wanting to call him Meathead. Is he doing it all, the carpentry and the painting?"

Mam surveyed the room. "He should be finished this week. I had to hire someone else to do the tile floor."

I swatted an errant buzzing torpedo. It was a great sun porch, even with detailing left undone. Mam already had placed her furniture "finds" from the estate sale. The bench in which she'd found the diary was now draped with an old aqua-and-red tablecloth to see if it would work as upholstery. She was going for a shabby chic look, although we'd always just thought of Nanny's screen porch as old-timey. It overlooked the old garage where as kids Mama and Aunt Boodie had jumped off the roof with umbrellas to break the fall. It didn't work. Aunt Boodie broke her leg and Mama the azalea bushes. I could see that Mam had put a cot out here just like then, only this mattress was covered in Sunbrella fabric. Maybe she wouldn't have to drag it in when it rained. God forbid a summer storm came up back then. We would wake in the night, shut all the windows, and pull in the cot mattresses off the porch. Then it would be too hot to sleep. The grownups had window fans, but we toughed it out until the rain stopped and we could open the door to the screen porch and breathe again. Nanny always said the best invention wasn't the phone or TV. It was the air conditioner. Amen.

"I see you went with yellow," I said. "Nice."

"J. T. suggested it, and I vetoed that," Mam said. "I thought he meant egg-yolk yellow, but then he said more like sweet corn, which isn't so bright."

Somehow, I wasn't surprised Mam used food instead of paint chips when decorating. I followed everyone through the open sliding door into Mam's den and its lovely cool air. "No mosquitoes got in here."

"But some dirt did, Mam. Chloe made a mess. Or Meatloaf, uh, Meatball," said Bonnie.

"Chloe has hardly been out today, and she doesn't track in that much." Mam puzzled over the pile of dirt on her gleaming hardwood floor while the possible culprit wagged her tail. She'd been asleep in her bed near the fireplace. "Besides, she went out the front before we left. And Meatball's very careful. He'd never leave a mess like this."

"Mama, I'm scared." Cissy's baby blues were even bigger than usual. "I think someone's been here."

"Don't be silly," Mam said. "I'm sure Chloe didn't let anyone in."

Bonnie and I looked at each other. Chloe might bark in welcome, but her bite was confined to Snausages.

"Yeah, let's just walk through each room to be sure." Bonnie got behind me and nudged me into the hall first. We moved from room to room on the first floor, flipping on lights.

"Everything looks accounted for," Bonnie whispered. "TV, DVR, computer—all here. You really should lock up from now on, Mam."

"Stop whispering," I said in a normal voice. "I think the

horse—if there was one—has left the barn. But she's right, Mam, about locking up when you leave and not just when you're home. It's not like it used to be, even if most break-ins are in the winter and they go for the vacant rentals."

"And construction sites," Mam noted. "The Culpeppers lost a bathtub, one of those fancy new ones that are supposed to look antique."

"I wonder if it's the one advertised on the bulletin board by town hall." I chuckled. "Remember, I told you about it. 'Claw-foot bathtub for sale. Fifty dollars. No feet.'"

Mam grinned. "Nobody better have made off with my spa tub, feet or no feet!" She led us toward the master suite in a single file—Mam, me, Bonnie (still pushing), Cissy, and Chloe at the tail end, literally. Her whole back end was wagging. Some watchdog.

"Only things of value in here would be my pearls and my diamond earrings," Mam said, opening her underwear drawer. "They're still here."

"Oh, great," said Bonnie. "That's the first place they'd look."

"Really?" Mam defended her hiding place. "I put them there so I won't forget where I put them. I can remember my underwear drawer. You know, you made me hide my Social Security card and voting registration after that identity theft thing, and now I don't remember where they are!" She looked at the partially open door to the walk-in closet, then flicked the light switch by reaching around the corner with her arm. The same arm reached up to a shelf. "J. T.'s gun's still here."

We all shuffled over to peer into the closet.

"How can you tell if anything's out of place?" Bonnie quipped.

"Can't," was all Mam said, although I noticed she kept staring at a pile of books on the floor.

There was nowhere to hide in the master bath. No shower curtain, thank goodness. Probably not a good time to bring up *Psycho*. Although Mam sounded in control, I knew it wasn't like her to give just a one-word answer. And why, as we backtracked, was she staring again at the pile of books?

I pulled her down the hall, following the others.

"Silver's here," Bonnie announced, opening the chest under Mam's antique china cabinet. She didn't have a real china cabinet, just an old washstand with doors and drawers that was Nanny's. Just recently, she had hung an old pie safe on the wall above it and started keeping her never-used crystal and often-used wineglasses in it. Several blue-and-white plates and a teapot were displayed on top. Very nice. I was getting tired of camping out in other people's houses.

"Wait," Mam said as she put on the brakes in the foyer by the stairs. We all bumped together like a freeway pileup. "Did you hear something upstairs?" This time, she was the one whispering.

We all froze, listening intently for what seemed an eternity but was probably all of forty seconds.

Cissy spoke first. "Mama, I'm scared."

"Should we leave or go up?" I asked, beginning to think that maybe retreat was the better part of valor. What if there was an intruder?

No one answered me. I could hear Mam breathing hard like she does when she starts getting claustrophobia. She avoids caves, tunnels, and even slow elevators. She let out a sigh. "Come on. I must have imagined the sound."

Bonnie pushed again, and I started up the stairs. Chloe decided to lie down on the bottom step.

Cissy refused to look in her room. "Just tell me if my computer's there. And check the closet, too."

"Computer's here," Bonnie said, then flung open the closet door "Gracious!"

"What?" asked Cissy, backing up.

"Nothing," Bonnie responded. "You just have a lot of clothes. Too short for anyone to hide behind, though." She grinned, and Cissy smiled weakly.

I dragged my hand along the white bead-board wainscoting. I guess I was thinking of support in case some surprised robber rushed past us for the stairs. I'd be trampled in the stampede, though, if we heard another sound. But there was nothing, no one.

"Well," said Mam, heading back down the stairs. Then she stopped suddenly, so we all bumped into each again as she let out a half-gasp, half-scream.

"Oh, my word!" Bonnie yelled in my ear. "What is it, Mam?"

Cissy's scream would have made Hitchcock proud. Everyone turned to run back up, but no one was moving. Then Chloe started howling as only Chloe can.

"Sorry," Mam yelped over Chloe's piteous cries. "I tripped over Chloe. There, there, girl. You're not hurt, even though you scared the daylights out of me."

"Out of all of us," I said, waiting for my heartbeat to return to normal.

"Good grief, Margaret Ann, did you think a burglar would be lying on the stairs?" said Bonnie.

"Possibly," said Mam, bending to pick up a Tupperware bowl in the hall as we headed for the kitchen. "Here, this is yours, Bonnie. Chloe was using it for a water dish."

"Why do I want this back?" Bonnie made a face.

"Because it doesn't belong to me," said Mam.

Bonnie rolled her eyes and put the bowl on the table. "Look, there's no one here. Mam, do you and Cissy want to come back home with me, since J. T. won't be back till tomorrow?"

"I don't know, maybe." Mam was looking into her pantry. "I still have a feeling somebody's been here. Those books in my to-be-read pile upstairs weren't in the order I left them, I don't think. And I don't remember my sewing box being on top of the dresser."

"Is that the sweet-grass basket like the one I have?" I asked. "I keep my everyday jewelry in mine."

"Where do you keep the good stuff, like Nanny's rings?" Bonnie wanted to know. "Not in your underwear drawer, I hope."

"No, Miss Smarty-Pants. They're in with my socks, so there." Enough of this folderol, time to be practical. "Listen, Mam, do you want to report a break-in? We could do it officially through dispatch, or I could call Will unofficially, although I need to warn you he's not real happy with us at the moment."

"Why not?" Bonnie was petting Chloe, who was snuffling around under the table like a furry Dustbuster in search of any crumbs. "He didn't look unhappy when we found you in the parking lot. Of course, his truck windows were kind of steamy."

"That was the A.C.," I retorted. "But I had to tell Will about us finding the diary and about Rabbit at the fish camp."

"Had to?" Mam asked. "What about Fort? What did you tell Will about him?"

"Just that Becky really disliked him, but don't worry. I didn't go into Julia or much detail. Just the stuff he already knew or was about to find out. Speaking of which, *Mam*"—I emphasized her name—"I thought we agreed not to talk about the cemetery with anyone. Who else did you tell besides Kathy Henderson?"

She smiled sheepishly. "Oh, not that many. I ran into Kathy at the Pig, and she and Beth Chestnut were talking in the produce aisle about your article, and I was looking at the bananas—I wanted them greener—and the cemetery came up."

Cissy, who had worked up the courage to visit the hall bath, returned. "What cemetery?" She picked up a banana from the fruit bowl on the counter. "This is too green to eat." Then she repeated, "What cemetery?"

"*The* cemetery," her mother stated. "Indigo Hill."

"Yeah, yeah, where all our people are, I know." Cissy was polishing an apple. "And where kids go hang out at the Colonel's tomb."

"You know about that?" Mam asked, one eyebrow raised.

"Everyone knows about it," Cissy said scornfully. "No big deal, y'know." She started to bite into the apple but quickly continued, "Not that I would ever go there, Mama."

"Humph, we never went there," Mam said.

"No," said Bonnie. "We just went to Red's back on Cry Baby Road, and the boys bought a pint of Canadian Mist, right, Mam?

We were too scared to leave the car. You just honked and this old woman bootlegger would come out—I guess she was Red—and you would pay through the car window."

"Boy, you couldn't do that today. I mean, it wouldn't be safe at all," said Mam. "Anyway, I only went there—to Red's, that is—a couple times. And I never drank and drove."

"She's right about that," quipped Bonnie. "J. T. wouldn't dare let you drive his car!"

Mam glared at her. "You can get your own wine, sister dear. But you'll have to convince Lindsey to drink Coke because I'm not driving you home. I'm going to have a glass of that good white, maybe two. I deserve it after tonight." She turned to me. "Maybe you should call Will unofficially."

"Rats!" Bonnie's outburst came out of nowhere. "Look, my teapot's gone." She showed the empty chain. "It must have fallen off again when I was at the fireworks. I know I had it on when we went because Wayne was asking me about it. Rats, rats, rats!"

"You can look for it in the morning, when it's light." Mam was consoling her, sort of. "Take the boys and tell them it's a treasure hunt."

Just then, the phone rang.

"Well, hey, Will," Mam said. "Lindsey was just going to call you. We've had a little excitement—" She stopped abruptly and handed the phone over. "He wants to talk to you."

"Everything okay?" Will sounded apprehensive.

"Oh, yeah, we're fine. It's just that it looks as if someone was here, but maybe not, because they didn't take anything, and there's no one here now but us chickies. Where are you?"

Will's voice was grim. "Miss Maudie's. There was a break-in at Middle House while she and her family were at the fireworks. And dispatch just called. The alarms have gone off at Pinckney."

May 21

I wonder if there is some way I can "lose" the lock on my locker at school and bring it home. It wouldn't work on my bedroom door, but I could put it on my trunk. That would help when Grandmother comes in here snooping, tho she says she's cleaning. She would want to know why I'm locking the trunk. Her trunk is locked. She keeps her jewelry box in there. She thinks I don't know where the key is, but I found it when I was trying to find the key to my bedroom that got "lost."

CHAPTER FIFTEEN

Miss Augusta, Get Your Gun, or Hot Pursuit

"Did you know Miss Augusta has a gun?"

"No," I told Will. It was the next morning, and I was leaning back in my creaky desk chair at Pinckney talking on the phone. "But I'm not surprised. Seems like everyone on this island has a gun of some kind. What does she have, a pearl-handled pistol?"

"Try a Colt .45 revolver. She said it belonged to her late husband, but she knows how to use it." Will couldn't disguise a note of admiration. But then he was all business again. "So you're sure everything's fine at Pinckney, nothing missing?"

"As far as I can tell, no one got inside the big house or Coach House. The alarms scared them, or else Miss Augusta threatening to shoot their heads off." I grinned at the vision of the plantation matriarch in her dressing gown and slippers pointing a revolver from a window.

"Lindsey, this is serious. That the only three reported break-ins last night were at Pinckney, Middle House, and Margaret Ann's makes you and your cousins the obvious connection. Somebody thinks you're still at Middle House. But what were they looking for?"

"Honest, Will, I don't know. Like I said, the only thing I can think of is the diary, but it was hidden in the bench, and Mam only found it by accident."

"But it was in the boat overnight, and Rabbit saw it."

"He didn't give any indication he knew what it was or that he read it. He was all about the shrimp dip."

"I know. You told me, and so did Margaret Ann." Will sounded weary, and no wonder. He'd been up all night coordinating crime scenes, listening to Mam, and disarming Miss Augusta. "I don't like the Rabbit connection."

I didn't either. Rabbit was dead, and I knew Will thought the circumstances were suspicious. Not that he'd told me. R. W. had traded me that tidbit this morning in exchange for my inside, off-the-record account of the break-ins. I hadn't told him about the diary. At least I didn't remember telling him in my pre-breakfast Coke haze, but then he had talked to Mam to get a quote. She'd been thrilled.

"Lindsey, you're awfully quiet."

"Sorry. I was thinking."

"Something I need to know?"

I hesitated for a split second. "No, but I'll call you if there's anything."

"Please do." Will started to say something, then interrupted himself. "Gotta go. Catch you later. Love you."

He hung up before I could reply. Had he just said the *L* word? Omigosh!

The remote rang almost immediately. Will?

"Pinckney Plantation. This is Lindsey."

Silence. Then a recorded message: "If you would like to make a call . . ." Good grief. If someone was dialing the plantation by accident, why didn't they just apologize, then hang up?

I got up and went into the kitchen—this was going to be a two-Coke day—and was almost trampled by Mam in full guide costume pushing through the connecting door from the dining room.

"Quick, get me some orange juice or ginger ale! I've got a fainter, and the husband says his wife is kinda diabetic." A summer guide had failed to show, so Mam was filling in.

I reached in the fridge and handed her a small can of juice. She grabbed it and rushed back to the front of the house. It never failed, especially in the summer heat. Folks with health issues would skip breakfast or lunch and then would feel lightheaded during a tour. If Mam was tending to the couple in the front parlor, where was the rest of the group? We like to keep a close eye on all "guests." Some of them don't have much in the way of manners. You never know what they might pick up or where they might wander to. They assume ropes don't apply to them.

The ringing phone called me back to the small office. "Pinckney Plantation. This is Lindsey," I said in my sweetest fake voice.

"It's Bonnie. I tried to call." Her voice was faint but emphatic. "Cell phones are cursed on this island."

"Yes, I know. And forget text messaging." I looked up as Mam swept in, collapsing in the chair opposite mine. She adjusted the hoop skirt so it wouldn't pop up as she leaned back. "Wait, let me put you on speakerphone so Mam can hear, too."

Mam leaned in close and all but shouted into the phone, "Did you find your teapot charm?"

Bonnie's voice came over the speaker. "No, and I looked everywhere, but—"

"Well, I told you to look where we sat last night," Mam interrupted. "And did you look in the car and in the clothes you had on? Maybe it got caught on that lacy top you were wearing."

"Wait, I need to tell you something before this blasted phone . . ." Bonnie's voice cut off.

I sighed. "She's on some island road where service is weak."

"She'll call back," Mam said confidently. "She did sound sort of keyed up or something."

"She's put out because when she finally got through, you

wouldn't let her get a word in edgewise!" I was overly familiar with the experience.

"Fine, I'll be quiet." Mam sat back with folded arms and trained her gaze on the speakerphone, as if her superpowers of communication extended to cell towers and beyond.

"While we're waiting, can I assume the orange juice revived our guest, and she's on her way home?"

Before she could answer, the remote in my hand rang yet again. Forgoing my manners in the certainty it was Bonnie, I said, "This is Lindsey, and you're back on speakerphone. Talk fast!"

Bonnie started in at top speed. "Now, just listen. I was pulling out of Oyster Creek Road onto the highway, and a U-Haul went zooming by in front of me. It had to slow down for the curve, and guess who was driving? Fort! With Gibbs Henry beside him in his Panama hat!" She rushed on. "They didn't see me, but suddenly it all became clear. Kinda like an epiphany! Lord. I just sounded like Cissy, didn't I?"

"What . . . ," Mam began, then frowned as the pen I threw hit her square on the forehead.

Bonnie didn't miss a beat. "Think about it. The only logical thing those two would be hauling in that truck would be furniture. If Gibbs is involved, it would be antiques. I'll betcha it's those pieces that supposedly burned in the fire. I think they were hiding them at the fish camp, including that partner's desk that I wanted." A trace of bitterness crept into the last comment. "Those two are trying to pull a fast one with the insurance company. You need to . . ." Her voice faded and then was cut off.

"Wow!" Mam said. "Just when you least expect it, Bonnie gets all smart on us."

I was a few thoughts ahead of her. "I sure hope she doesn't try to follow them." Bonnie didn't need to be pursuing Fort in his present state of mind. As I'd just said, practically everybody on Indigo has a gun, and a good ol' boy like Fort would have several. "Mam, drop that hoop skirt and let's go find her!" I headed out the back door.

Mam's voice followed me. "You better have your cell, because Bonnie's got mine. Her carrier doesn't work here."

"Big surprise. Come on!"

Mam caught up with me on the path, having discarded the hoop part of her costume to reveal shorts underneath. The purple ruffled top would have to remain for the moment. "I'll drive," she said, realizing her Tahoe was blocking me in. Hunched behind the wheel of the huge SUV, Mam flew down the back gravel drive as I tried to reach Bonnie on the phone. I finally got through as we turned onto the open road.

"Please tell me you're not following that U-Haul truck." I started right in. "Where are you?"

"Crossing the bridge on the way to Centerville. Fort's a car and truck in front of me."

Well, she couldn't make a U on the bridge. "Mam and I are a few minutes behind you. We think you should stop at the River Road turn and wait for us. Don't try to confront Fort or anything. We know he's got a mean streak, and he may have killed Rabbit."

Bonnie's voice was calm. "I'm just following the truck. And it's too late to stop at River Road. We both just turned on it, going toward the Savannah Highway. They must be going to Charleston."

"What is she saying?" Mam's eyes were on the road. "I hope she's stopping because it looks like a yacht's on the waterway, and they'll be closing the bridge in a sec."

"Step on it!"

She complied, and we were on the bridge and through the crossing gate even as the red lights started flashing. I'm sure the bridge keeper was cursing us as we rumbled across, but he waited to close the mainland gate in our lane. We bounced when we hit the causeway, where oncoming traffic was already backing up.

"Bonnie, we're over the bridge, and we'll turn on River Road. Where are you? I'm putting you on speaker. Mam's having a hissy fit."

"Am not!" she shouted. "Bonnie, can you hear me? Put your

cell on speaker, too. You need to have both hands free in case you need to protect yourself."

"Cool it, I'm already on speaker. You need two hands to drive this curvy road. Why don't you call Will or Olivia, Lindsey, and tell them about Fort?"

"Because I'm on the phone with you, and I'm not getting off until you turn around or we find you."

"No place to turn," Bonnie said blithely. "Nothing's going to happen. Uh-oh. I take that back."

"What? What?" Mam and I both demanded.

"We're stopped at the railroad crossing, and there's a freight train with about fifty million freight cars going by. Fort is stopped in front of me, and I think he saw me in his rearview mirror." She paused. "Yep, he's getting out of his truck and walking back this way. Maybe I should roll down my window and act all surprised and nicey-nice."

"No! Lock your doors right now, Bonnie Lynn!" Mam was breaking out in a sweat. "And whatever you do, don't say anything about stolen antiques." Why did Mam always feel she had to shout at a phone?

"Too late. I already hit the window button, and from the look on his face, he just heard you on my phone." Bonnie's voice rose. "Well, hey, Fort! I didn't realize that was you up there. Can you get over how long this train is? Since there's no one behind me, I'm thinking about turning around and going the back way over by Toogoodoo."

Fort's voice wasn't as loud, but his words and tone were clear. "That might be a good idea. I'll follow you for a while, instead of the other way around."

Mam started to lean into the phone, but I put my hand over it. Consequently, neither one of us heard Bonnie's reply. Then Bonnie said, "I'm backing up, girls, and making a three-point road turn. Looks like Fort is going to do the same. Good grief, as if he could keep up with me in that truck!" Bonnie acted like her minivan was a racecar.

I grabbed the phone as it started to fly off the seat when Mam made a quick right on Toogoodoo, heading toward the intersection with River Road. People from "off" used it all the time to get to the highway and Charleston because it looked like a shortcut on the map. But locals knew it had a couple of speed traps and lots of deer. "We're not far away from you. Is he really following you?"

"Yep, and that truck can go faster than I thought. Don't get off the line with me, in case he tries to run me off the road." Bonnie started talking to herself. "How can that stupid oaf be gaining on me?"

Her voice started to break up, so we could only hear bits of her monologue: "Closer . . . shining . . . crap . . . a gun, no way . . . I'm gonna pull over in this new . . . missed me . . ." Static drowned out the rest. Then came a sharp squeal, followed by several expletives.

"Bonnie, Bonnie!" Mam yipped. "We lost you. Oh, Bonnie, word-I-can't-say!"

"Bonnie's sure saying them." I found her unaccustomed profanity somewhat reassuring. At least she was alive and talking. But then even the static stopped. I turned to Mam. "Look for a new building or house along this stretch of road. She said she was going to pull over."

"Nothing but woods and fields and the old filling station," Mam said. "There's not even another car in sight!"

"I know, but keep looking. She can't be that far away."

We sped by weed-filled ditches. Had she really said *gun*? Then we rounded a curve.

"Look, there's a new car wash!" I pointed to a concrete-block building not yet open for business. "Turn here! This has to be it!"

Mam pulled in the paved parking area and braked to a screeching stop as Uncle James's new car emerged from the overhang. Water spots on its gleaming exterior indicated that the drying cycle wasn't yet operational.

Bonnie got out the driver's door looking as mad as a wet hen— and just as wet. Her hair and clothes were dripping. She jerked open Mam's car door with some choice words about defective sunroofs. "Get in the backseat, Mam, I'm driving," she ordered. "Pass me that old towel, too. And here, this doesn't belong to me." She tossed her sister the waterlogged phone.

"I swear, Bonnie Lynn, Daddy is going to have a dying-duck fit when he sees what you did to his new car!" Mam leaned over the seat just as Bonnie tried to slide it back to accommodate her longer legs. "Hey, watch it!"

"I wouldn't have needed it if the van hadn't woken with a flat tire this morning. But Daddy won't ever know unless you tell him," Bonnie cautioned as she swerved the Tahoe toward the exit. "I got soggier than the car did while I was trying to figure how to work that stupid sunroof. I didn't even know it was partly open until one of those blue octopus fringe things slapped me in the face."

"I still don't see why you decided to wash the car." Mam was mopping her phone with her shirttail.

"I didn't!" Bonnie burned rubber as she turned left. "I pulled in back so Fort would go past and not see me, and I guess I triggered some sprayer device." The car accelerated. "At least there wasn't any soap."

"Where are we going?" I asked, punching Will's number on my cell phone and praying I could get service.

"I saw them turn down the road to the Christmas-tree farm." Bonnie's hands gripped the steering wheel. "I want to know where they're taking my partner's desk!"

"You don't have to yell!" Mam shouted.

I could barely hear Will's voice as I began recapping recent events in what I hoped were concise and semi-coherent terms. "You did tell me to call you if there was anything," I said, quickly wrapping things up. "I know you think we jump to conclusions, Will, but Bonnie thinks she saw a gun and . . ."

Static cut me off, too, but not before I heard, "Stop!" Did he mean me talking or us driving? The sisters were still bickering back and forth. Mam was telling Bonnie to slow down, and Bonnie was telling her to shut up. And now there was a siren. Great, we were being stopped for speeding.

Bonnie glared at Mam. "Don't say a word. Let me do the

talking." She rolled down her window.

Mam muttered darkly, "Registration's in the glove compartment."

I looked in the side mirror at the patrol car parked behind us. Maybe it was Will or Olivia or Earl Crosby, who has known us since kindergarten. Nope. Surprise, surprise, it was none other than my kindergarten cop, Officer Walters. The conscientious young fellow appeared to take his job very seriously.

"Driver's license and registration, please," he said with brisk efficiency. "You were doing sixty in a fifty zone back there. What's the rush?"

Bonnie showed him her damp wallet. He eyed her wet hair and clothes.

"Are you all right"—he looked down at her license—"Ms. Tyler?"

"Well, as you can see, I'm just a wee bit wet." Bonnie's Southern accent would have done Scarlett proud. "I left the sunroof open in my daddy's car as I went through the car wash. Stupid thing to do, I know. Thank goodness, my sister and cousin were driving by and, well . . ." Her honeyed voice trailed off in hopes he would be satisfied with that half-baked explanation.

He turned his attention to me as I passed over the registration. Mam was in the backseat, her hand to her mouth, looking ready to pop.

"How are you today, Ms. Fox?"

"Fine, Officer Walters, just fine," I replied sweetly. "And yourself?"

He nodded, appearing to come to the conclusion that the less he asked us, the better. He stepped back and started writing in his book. He handed back Bonnie's license and the registration, along with a ticket.

"It's just a warning because you weren't fifteen miles over, but let's take it a little slower from now on, ladies."

Mam couldn't stand it. "We only were in a hurry to catch some thieves!"

Officer Walters paused, then thought better of it and walked slowly back to his cruiser, shaking his head as he went.

"Well, he didn't seem to be the least bit interested in apprehending any criminals." Mam sighed heavily. "I hope you had better luck with Will, Lindsey. What did he say?"

I sidestepped the question. No need to let them know I hadn't really heard what he said. But I had a pretty good idea. "It's best if we go home and let the sheriff's department handle things from here."

"But—" Mam said.

"No arguing," Bonnie intervened. "Straight home, do not pass Go, except for me to rescue Daddy's car."

"I know someone in Centerville where you can get it professionally cleaned," I said.

Mam wouldn't let go of our adventure. She was like a Lab puppy with a chew toy. "What exactly did Will say?" she asked.

" 'Stop!' " I said, which was true. "We need to go home and let the law handle it." Thinking back on it, Will hadn't interrupted my account, which made me think Fort's insurance scam was already on his radar.

Bonnie tried to wrest Mam's attention. "I'll buy you a new phone, one with a camera in it so you can take pictures of your flower arrangements."

"But—" Mam wanted the last word.

Bonnie had it, though. "I think Officer Walters is kinda cute. Did you see that dimple?"

June 6

Grandmother gave me a watch for graduation. F. gave me a $50 bill to buy whatever I want, but Grandmother said I should use it to buy my bus ticket when I go to Mississippi to visit this summer. I hate taking anything from F., but Grandmother was right there, so I just said thank you. They don't know my real plans, that going to see Mama's family will be my cover story so I can go to Canada with J. and R. We are going to wait until August, before he is supposed to report to the army and J. is supposed to go to some music festival in New York. We will drive her Mustang to Montreal, and by the time anyone knows we aren't where they think, we will be safe. R. will be safe. That's the most important thing.

CHAPTER SIXTEEN

The Queen of Diamonds

"Did Miss Augusta say why she wanted to see us?" asked Bonnie. "Will did take that gun away from her, didn't he?" Bonnie was a little paranoid after yesterday's car chase.

It was Wednesday afternoon, and we three were trekking over to the Coach House, where Miss Augusta was having tea with Pinckney's lawyer, Ross Savage. Despite his name, he was a mild-mannered man except in court. There, he was known as "the Velvet Hammer" because his opposition never knew what hit them until it was too late.

Since we were expected, we just knocked and walked right into the sitting area.

"Welcome, girls. I'm sure you know Mr. Savage." Miss Augusta made the introductions.

The white-haired attorney stood to greet us, neat as a pin in his summer-weight seersucker suit, complete with a red bow tie and white buc shoes—the accepted Charleston lawyer uniform. He gave a reserved smile as he offered his hand to each of us. He made me feel grubby, even though I was wearing a khaki skirt and top that had started the day wrinkle free.

Miss Augusta, as cool as a cucumber in green linen, was sitting upright in her recliner, so the chair looked like a regular wingback. She waved as from a throne. "Margaret Ann, will you please bring in a dining-room chair? Bonnie and Lindsey can sit on the love seat. Mr. Savage has a most interesting story to tell you. He also represents the Bailey family."

From what we'd heard, Fort needed a good lawyer right about now. Both he and Gibbs Henry had been arrested yesterday when they arrived at the North Charleston storage unit Gibbs had rented. The U-Haul truck, which as we suspected was full of Comfort's End antiques supposedly lost in the fire, had been seized and the partners in crime carted off to jail to face charges that included arson and insurance fraud. The district attorney would likely be charging Fort with manslaughter as soon as the investigation into Rabbit's death was complete. After a night in the pokey, both Fort and Gibbs had posted bail this morning, although no one knew where the funds had come from. Alas, Bonnie's partner's desk would be held in a county warehouse as evidence for the time being.

Mr. Savage appeared to read our minds. "I've retired from criminal law," he said. "My son will be handling Mr. Bailey's case. But I am in charge of his late mother's estate, and that's why I came to see Miss Augusta today."

Miss Augusta nodded regally. "It's about the Comfort-Bailey family jewels."

Bonnie's elbow nudged me in the side, but I didn't dare look at her or Mam. That "family jewels" had another connotation apparently hadn't occurred to Miss Augusta.

She continued. "When Mr. Savage and Fort accessed the Bailey safe-deposit box last week, not all of the jewels were there."

"What was missing?" Mam leaned forward.

"Let me explain." The lawyer calmly addressed us. "The famous diamond teardrops were there but not another diamond with a most unique history. Tell me, are any of you familiar with the British queen Charlotte of Mecklenburg?"

Everyone looked at me. After all, I had lived in Charlotte, "the Queen City," in Mecklenburg County, North Carolina.

"She was married to King George III, who was king during the Revolutionary War—he lost the colonies," I said. "They had, like, fifteen children, one of whom became the prince regent, and then George IV."

Mr. Savage nodded his approval. "Anything else?"

I felt like I was taking an exam in British history. "Helen Mirren played her in the movie *The Madness of King George*, with Nigel Hawthorne as George."

Mam piped up. "Mad King George. He was crazy, right?"

"He acted like it at times, but now they think he suffered from porphyria, which is a metabolic disorder." I looked at Mam. "I think it's inherited."

She replied sagely. "Insanity runs in families. We just have to hope that Cousin Bitsy is it from our generation. Of course, she doesn't think she's crazy, but I think anyone who raises monkeys in a motor home has to be bananas. She dresses them in little outfits."

Miss Augusta sniffed to remind us that we were not there to discuss chimpanzees or their wardrobes. "Queen Charlotte?"

I dredged up some more trivia. "She was German and unpopular. She wasn't especially pretty, maybe even homely. George was supposed to have been disappointed when he met her after his mother picked her out as his bride, although he was hardly a picture himself, if you go by the portraits. Plump, red faced, and googly eyed. But presumably they were happy together."

"I'll say," Bonnie said. "All those children!"

Mr. Savage's thin lips lifted in what he probably thought was a smile. Or maybe it was a grimace. "George was a misunderstood monarch in many ways, and you are correct, Lindsey, in that the English did not take well initially to Queen Charlotte. She also had some enemies within the rest of the royal family, which brings us to today's subject. The queen had numerous jewels—her wedding dress was covered with pearls and diamonds—and she also was given many precious gems, including the very large and exquisite

Arcot diamonds, which were a gift from an Indian nawab. These included five brilliants, one of which was an oval of more than thirty-eight carats."

Mam's eyes widened at the vision of such a hefty rock. "How did Miss Eliza get that big a diamond?"

"Oh, she didn't," Mr. Savage said quickly. "I'm sorry if I gave you the impression that she did. No, no, the Arcots have their own history, as they were sold and split up after Charlotte's death. Her son, disregarding his mother's will, took one for his crown. Others passed into the hands of British and German aristocracy and were recut and reset. I believe an Arab sheik owns one that's on a necklace. He bought it at auction." Mr. Savage paused and took a sip of iced tea before continuing. "It was at another auction, at Christie's in 1819, the year after Queen Charlotte's death, that the majority of her personal possessions, including jewelry and trinkets, were sold. Miss Eliza's records indicate that one of her ancestors, Joseph Comfort, bought a 'splendid' diamond and several silver pieces."

Miss Augusta was growing impatient. "What Ross—Mr. Savage—is trying to tell you is that he and Fort think that a particular piece of jewelry once belonging to Queen Charlotte ended up in the estate sale by mistake. May we see your teapot charms, please?"

Mam and I looked at Bonnie, who shifted uncomfortably on the love seat. "Mam's is the largest," she said.

Mam leaned forward again and pulled her teapot charm on its chain out for inspection. "It does look like a Georgian teapot, I guess. But I thought that was the point of reproductions."

The lawyer peered with a magnifying glass at the chubby charm in Mam's hand. "This one is a reproduction. There's no hallmark."

"Lindsey's has lots of filigree," Bonnie suggested.

Miss Augusta pursed her lips when she saw my silver teapot charm nestling next to my silver gator. "Really, Lindsey."

"A very pretty trinket," Mr. Savage said, "but also a reproduction."

"Bonnie?" Miss Augusta inquired.

"I don't have mine with me today," she said. She cleared her throat. "Actually, Miss Augusta, I seem to have misplaced it."

The ensuing silence was broken, naturally, by Mam. "Admit it, Bonnie, you've lost Queen Charlotte's diamond."

July 12

Another letter came today from Queens College with a form so they can match me with a roommate. Even if I wasn't going to Canada, I wouldn't want to go to an all-girls school in Charlotte where they lock you in at night. Grandmother said she wouldn't pay for me to go anywhere else, and I should be grateful I am going to college. When she decided all this last fall, I went along because at least it was a way to leave Indigo. Now, it is moot. I am going to be with R. far, far away. I can hardly wait. The days drag, and it is so hot.

Chapter Seventeen

Lost and Found

"So now we know why Miss Eliza always played diamonds," Mam said cheerfully. J. T. was home from his mancation, her freezer was full of fish he'd caught—or claimed to have caught— and all was right with her world.

"I suppose," I said. "But we don't know much more than that." I flicked on the ceiling fan in my office. Thursday morning was starting out to be another scorcher. "Any word from Bonnie on the second search?"

"No. She took her boys and little Chad out to the bridge landing for a treasure hunt, and from there she's taking them all to the Vacation Bible School picnic out at the Point." Mam sat down in "her" chair and propped her feet on my desk. No hoop skirt today, but her gift-shop shift started at noon.

"Be happy you're here and not roasting hot dogs in the sun," I told her. "They're the ones who are going to cook. There's not any shade to speak of."

In my mind, I pictured the jetty of land where the river emptied into St. Helena Sound. The shifting sands had been kind to that length of beach, which stretched like a glaring sheet in the sun at low tide. It was a favorite setting for gatherings when the weather was good. But in the summer, only mad dogs, Englishmen, and apparently Baptists braved the noonday sun.

"Mam," I asked, "if VBS finished last week, why is the picnic today instead of last Thursday?"

"Something to do with a family reunion that booked the park for the whole day way back in the winter." Mam was idly flipping through a copy of *South Carolina Wildlife*. She always had to be doing something, and it was driving her crazy that she only had church flowers to do this week. "Think it might have been the Kinseys and the Hiotts. We're related somehow. But Aunt Cora's the expert on cousin removal."

I grinned. "You make her sound like a vacuum cleaner or some kind of paid assassin."

Mam made a face. "I think there are a few kinfolk she could do without. She couldn't go because she trotted off to that church retreat."

"We missed our chance to quiz her about the curse of the Comforts." I was supposed to touch base with R. W. today about my history column for next week, although he might want to delay it again while he chronicled Fort's latest misadventures. Hard to believe it had just been a week since the estate sale. Which reminded me. "Want to look at the yearbooks and see if we can decipher any more diary stuff?" I asked Mam.

Part of me wanted her to say no. Becky's diary, even reading between the lines, wasn't all that edifying or entertaining, although she'd probably be mortified at strangers reading her most private thoughts.

Mam tuned into my thoughts. "I don't want to even read *my* diary from high school. How embarrassing! Do you suppose teens still have real diaries, or do they all do blogs anyone can read? Cissy and Ashley do one together. So much for secrets. Do you still keep a journal?"

"Not so much. Too tired. Also, looking back on it, I mostly wrote when I was unhappy, relentlessly analyzing all the relationships that went wrong and renewing my feminist ideals."

Mam studied me. "It's your bad-boy fixation. That's why Will's good for you. He's a good guy. You better not wreck it."

"He is a good guy, and what makes you think I'm going to wreck it?" There were times—and this was one of them—when I'd like to have some secrets that belonged just to me.

"I know you," Mam said in that cheery way that was starting to get on my nerves. "You're commitment phobic, and have been ever since college and your one-minute marriage. You let a guy get only so close, and then you dump him before he walks out on you."

"Which saves time," I said moodily. Even though Mam didn't know about Will breaking up with me in college—or that we even had hooked up back then—she was uncomfortably close to the truth about me and men. I had an affinity for emotionally unavailable guys, and if one by chance started getting serious, I turned and ran. But this time, I didn't want to run. Did I?

For once, Mam decided not to explore my psyche further. The magazine slid from her lap as she stood. "I'm going to get some of Marietta's oatmeal cookies for us. You get the yearbooks and your copy of the diary. I think we should do a clue map. That usually helps."

A clue map. Mam has never gotten over reading Nancy Drew. Now, all the TV crime shows she watches and the mysteries we all love fuel her desire to do some detecting. I rationalize my own curiosity—and risk Will's disapproval—by telling myself I am still a reporter at heart. A marvelous excuse to be nosy.

As each day went by, the reality of finding Becky's bones was fading. She was becoming a character in a book, an intriguing subject for a newspaper or magazine article. We knew as much about her as long-ago Queen Charlotte, maybe less. Had Becky, for example, known about the jeweled charm? Did she perhaps identify with Charlotte, another outsider? Was her dislike of her grandmother just a case of teenage rebellion or something more? And what about her relationship with her uncle?

We knew now that Fort and Gibbs had been searching for the missing charm. It was likely Fort didn't even know about the diary. I remembered the heated conversation between Fort and Wayne at the fireworks. If Wayne's father had been Becky's dentist, Wayne was the one with her dental records. But did they keep the records of dead people? Everybody assumed Becky's body had been swept away in Hurricane Camille. No one knew she was in a makeshift grave on Indigo. No one but whoever buried her . . .

Mam had two glasses of iced tea in her hands. "I folded the cookies in napkins in my pockets. Hope they're not too crumbly. I think we should start heading things out like usual. You have a pen?"

I traded a ballpoint and the back of a blank work order for tea and cookie crumbs.

"Okay, we figured out that J. is Julia." Mam was already writing. "This column is for all the people who could be R. The yearbooks can be our reference guide."

"They're only going to help us with Becky's classmates," I pointed out. "What if R. didn't go to Granville High?"

Mam was unfazed. "I said 'guide.' At least it's a starting point. I've been writing down names from her class and the ones right ahead and right behind. Randy Roe was two years ahead, but I think we can rule him out. He was surprised at the graveyard, or else he deserves an Oscar."

"Who else?" I asked.

"Ray Simmons was a class behind, and his brother Ron was a class ahead. Ravenel Hampton was in Ray's class, and Rabbit was in Becky's. I bet he was socially promoted. What does he look like in the yearbook?"

I recognized Rabbit's ferret face. "Like himself, only lots younger and cleaner. No sports or clubs listed. His real name was Robert Hare, Jr." I turned back to Becky's senior picture, the one in which Mam thought she looked sad. To my mind, she appeared distant, detached from the draped collar and fake pearls all the senior girls wore for their pictures. "Becky was in the National Honor Society, French Club, Drama Club, and yearbook."

"I definitely don't see her with Rabbit," Mam put in. "He was too dorky. Are there any other pictures of her? Check the index."

"Here's the yearbook staff." I pointed out the picture to Mam. "Julia's standing in the back with another teacher, Ralph McDonald. He must have been the other faculty adviser."

"Ralph!" Mam exclaimed. "Maybe he was R. Becky had a thing for an older man."

I shot down Mam's idea. "Way too old. He looks like he's ready to retire. Becky's R. was draft age, remember?"

"Is that R. W. slouching in the front row? He sure had a lot more hair!" Mam peered closer. "He's cute, though, like somebody in one of those boy bands—the Dave Clark Five, or maybe Paul Revere and the Raiders."

"Not the Stones, though," I said. "Not that gritty. He's sitting next to Wally Smith and Kathy Henderson, only she was Kathy Hutto then. She doesn't look so different now, just older, and her hair is better."

"Everybody's hair is better, if they still have it," Mam commented. "You can hardly see Becky's face, between her long hair and the way she's standing behind that beehive girl. It's interesting to see how the times were a-changing from the clothes and hair. Some of the guys—the jocks with letter jackets, mostly, like Wally—still have short hair, but others are letting it grow. The girls are all still wearing skirts and dresses, no slacks or jeans. Look, Kathy's got on a Villager blouse, but she's wearing a peace-symbol necklace and hoop earrings. Weird."

Something else was weird about the pictures in the yearbook. Then it hit me. All the faces were white. Granville High hadn't yet integrated.

"What if," I proposed, "R. went to the black high school?"

"Then he'd be black," Mam said.

"Duh. But wouldn't Miss Eliza and Fort have had a conniption if Becky was seeing a black guy?"

"That would be a major secret," Mam confirmed. "Wow! Maybe that's it."

"Posey might know," I said. "He went to Granville, but he has older brothers and sisters. We could ask him, or Olivia."

"Olivia's way younger than us," Mam noted, "and Marietta's too old."

"Marietta too old for what?" The housekeeper stood with arms akimbo in the office doorway. "I don't care if you grown, I still can slap your fannies, you misbehave on me or make a mess." She surveyed my desk and shook her head. "I don't see how you know where anything is."

"It's not dirty, just piley." I defended my stacks of papers and books. "I collect things."

"You collecting dust." She ran a finger down the doorjamb and frowned. "You pick up in here now and I'll bring you the furniture polish. That dog of yours been on the chair again, and that throw rug a disgrace. Vacuum cleaner in the hall closet, in case you forgot. Margaret Ann, get them schoolbooks off the floor. What you doing with them old things anyway?"

"Research for Lindsey's next history column." Mam looked up from her notes. "It's about some stuff from the sixties. Do you remember if there were any interracial couples on Indigo?"

"In the 1960s?" Marietta's eyebrows almost hit her hairline. "Do, Jesus, they none much on the island now. You grew up here, you know that. Folks get along, work together, but they don't mix much. Like go with like. Not saying it ought to be that way, but that the way it is, mostly."

Mam nodded. She wanted everyone to be as color-blind as she was, but she also was realistic. All of us knew, too, that class divided the island as much as color. Education has been an equalizer. Granville High is one of the best schools in the state, which admittedly still lags behind much of the country. That's the reason both well-to-do blacks and whites like to use so they can send their kids to parochial and private schools. The only railroad tracks on the island are imaginary, but there are still areas on the "wrong" side. Rutted dirt roads snake off into the jungly woods, then suddenly give way to clusters of old wooden houses and rusty trailers where poverty is as rampant as kudzu.

"Like go with like," Mam repeated. "Remember how Nanny

always advised us it was just as easy to fall in love with a rich man as a poor one? But then she'd laugh because she hadn't. 'Money has a way of marrying money,' she'd say."

"True, true," Marietta said, chuckling. "Mr. Bennie not have much till he won that lottery ticket. Then he go and marry that widow from Adam's Run with more money than sense. But they both homely, bless their hearts." She paused, then said seriously, "I worry 'bout that sister of yours. She is too pretty for her own good."

So Marietta had noticed, too. Mam and I had concluded that in addition to losing the diamond, Bonnie had lost her marbles.

"Raging hormones," Mam said. "You know any anti-love potions?"

"Humph." Marietta was not amused. "That ring on her finger ought to be enough. Dr. Wayne a nice man—good looks, lots of money. But he know better, too. He is not for her."

I agreed, but I also picked up on something else. "Wayne has money?"

"More than he know what to do with," Marietta said. "His mama and daddy both got it from their families. He an only child, so it all came to him. When he a boy, they call him Richie, on 'count of he named for his daddy, Richard Wayne. Everyone else call him that 'cause he so rich. My sister used to clean for his mama. He was spoil rotten and acted it until he came back from that war. He was Wayne from then on, and he change more than his name. Went back to school and to church. He a deacon now."

Marietta stopped. "I almost forgot why I come back here. Bonnie forgot the oatmeal cookies for the picnic. *My* cookies that she ask for special for Ben and Sam! I put 'em in tins on the kitchen table. One of you, go take them out there to her. I gotta finish the chicken salad for Miss Augusta's lunch." She called back over her shoulder as she marched off. "You can have some when you come back."

She swished away, not knowing the bombshell she had dropped on us.

"Lindsey?"

"Okay, Mam, we'll both go." I grabbed my purse. "You go get the sandwiches while I lock this office."

"Surely, there is nothing wrong with Wayne. I mean he . . . Oh, my goodness." She was out the door, talking all the while. And she was still babbling when I met her in the driveway. "I thought of nicknames, like Red Sanders, although he's too young, but I forgot first names."

"Maybe I should drive."

"No. Here, take these cookies and this copy of the notebook. Get in, I'm driving." When Mam gets flustered, she gets bossy. Okay, bossier. "While you're riding, look back over the entries where it seems like she's scared of someone." She whizzed out the drive on what seemed like two wheels. "I hope it's not Wayne, uh, Richie she was afraid of. That can't be right. She loved him. Hurry, Lindsey, look for more clues."

"You know I can't read while I'm riding. I'll get carsick." I turned the A.C. on full blast. "And stop with this crazy driving."

"I feel like I am going crazy," Mam said as she stomped on the accelerator.

"You don't have far to go," I said.

"Huh? It's fifteen miles to the Point!"

"I know that! You said you were going crazy, and I said you don't have far to go. Calm down. And slow down."

She eased off the gas, then yelled, "Get out of the way, you stupid tomato truck!"

"Don't pass, Mam!" I yelled back. "There's a car—"

"I see it," she said, braking. "What are you thinking, cousin?"

"You mean besides you trying to get us killed?" I clutched the sliding cookie tins. "I'm thinking that Wayne knows more than he's telling."

"I'd call Bonnie, but she can't get a signal." Mam gripped the steering wheel. "As soon as we get there, I want you in reporter mode. Call him Richie and see what he does. And don't let him off the hook, Lois Lane!"

I braced against the dashboard as we slid around a curve. "Yes, ma'am, Mam!"

CHAPTER EIGHTEEN
Undertow

Mam had to slow down as we passed the pavilion on the Front Beach Road. Not only was the speed limit thirty-five, but cars, trucks, and SUVs were parked higgledy-piggledy on both sides of the street, which was lined with white-trimmed beach cottages, beach houses, and beach mansions in every shade of the rainbow. Fourth of July week, and Indigo's beach was packed, every house full to overflowing. American flags flew from porches, along with the blue, garnet, and orange insignias of the Citadel, South Carolina, and Clemson. Surfboards were propped against railings draped with neon towels, and beachgoers clumped at crosswalks, toting umbrellas, coolers, and assorted paraphernalia.

"Look at all the people!" Mam marveled. "I forget how crowded it gets down here. That little boy is going to wish he'd worn Crocs or flip-flops. Look at him jumping on the sidewalk. I don't know how he's going to make it over the asphalt. Be like walking on hot coals. Doesn't he have a mother?"

"She's probably the one in the thong with the sunburned back," I said. "Ye gods! Some people!"

Mam concentrated on driving, watching out for darters. I could see the turnoff to the Point up ahead, the sandy drive shaded by palmettos. Good luck finding a parking place, though. I started to say something about a sun-yellow Hummer taking up two spaces, but we weren't exactly in a Mini.

Just then, a gold minivan vacated its spot.

"We'll have to hike in," Mam said, maneuvering the Tahoe. "But we aren't likely to get much closer. Don't forget your hat."

The air enveloped us like a wet blanket smelling of sun, salt, and Hawaiian Tropic. My sunglasses fogged up, and I tripped against Mam, who had stopped to shake a sand spur out of her sandal. The gold minivan was having a hard time getting around the circle to exit.

"Is that an EMS truck up there?" I said.

"May just be here as a precaution, or else maybe someone got stung by a jellyfish and didn't have any meat tenderizer with them." Mam strode ahead of me, winding around fenders and stepping high to avoid more stickers. "Or someone could be sick from the sun. People from off just don't understand they need to drink lots of water in this heat."

I slapped at a black fly on my arm and followed her from the parking area to the path leading over a small dune to the beach. It was almost low tide, and dark green wavelets licked at the sand, trimming it with creamy foam.

But the crowd we came upon wasn't relaxing in chairs or on towels. They were standing and pointing at the water. Dolphins? A shark? Fishermen caught hammerheads and sand sharks all the time, but I didn't see anyone fishing.

Mam's steps quickened. "Something's wrong," she said, passing a woman holding onto a struggling toddler even as she gazed seaward. "Hurry!" she gasped. "I want to find Bonnie and the boys."

I trotted faster. This can't be good, I thought, scanning the sand ahead. A throng of people faced the water, but a smaller group huddled to one side, two EMS guys in the middle. "Mam, look!"

I'd spotted Bonnie's hot-pink cover-up. She was tightly clutching Ben while a sobbing Sam stood next to her, a towel around his shoulders, his dripping Hawaiian swim trunks riding low on his hips. One of the med techs was kneeling over a slight figure lying on the sand. Oh, no! Chad Henderson?

"Tell me, tell me! What's happened?" Mam dropped to her knees and reached for Sam, who became an octopus, grabbing at both of us with arms and legs. I looked over his squirming shoulder at Bonnie. Tears tracked down her face. Her mouth opened and she gulped air, but only a sob escaped the trembling lips. Chad was sitting up now, thank goodness, heavy coughs racking his chest. Bonnie tried again to say something but gave up. She buried her face in Ben's wet hair. His face was buried in her neck. He was quiet, too quiet. Violent shivers shook his small frame. Bonnie tightened her arms around him.

"What happened?" I asked an EMS guy, who was watching his partner rub down Chad with a towel. The color was coming back in the boy's face, and he had stopped coughing.

"He'll be fine," the wiry tech assured me in a relaxed manner. Guess it was part of his training. "Just swallowed some water and got scared. He and this other little fellow"—he gestured at Ben—"went out too far after a wave snatched their float. The current must of grabbed hold, and they couldn't make it back to the shallow part on their own." He stopped, and his eyes shifted to the beach and back again. "Her friend," he pointed to Bonnie. "He saw what was happening and went after them. He grabbed the boys and put them on the float and shoved them back toward the beach." He again looked apprehensively toward the ocean.

This time, through a gap in the crowd, I saw rescue personnel on Jet Skis. They were about thirty yards offshore, slowly motoring back and forth parallel to the beach. I stood up, gently disentangling Sam, who immediately clamped onto Mam. She soothed him under her breath. "There, there."

"The friend?" I asked. "Where is he?"

Bonnie's head jerked, and there was panic in her voice. "They haven't found him yet?" She clambered to her feet, still holding Ben. "Wayne is still out there!"

The tech placed a comforting hand on her arm. "They're still looking, don't worry."

Mam and I looked at each other. We knew how treacherous the undertow could be. She stood up, Sam hanging onto her leg.

"He has to be there! He saved Ben and Chad's life!" Bonnie was on the verge of hysterics. "Please keep looking! Please!"

"Bonnie Lynn!" Mam snapped. "Stop it this minute! You're scaring the boys. Heck, you're scaring me and Lindsey. Pull yourself together." She enfolded all of us in a group hug. Mam's good in a crisis. "There, there," she whispered. "There, there."

❀

Four hours later, I opened Aunt Boodie and Uncle James's back screen door. "Come on in," I said.

Olivia nodded and ducked in. I knew from her sweat-stained uniform and solemn expression that the search-and-rescue mission was now search and recovery.

She crossed the tile floor and pulled out the barstool next to mine. I poured her a glass of iced tea. She took a long drink, then sighed. "I am so sorry."

"I know. We all are." The tea eased my own scratchy throat.

"Where's Bonnie?" she asked.

"She and the boys are asleep in the back bedroom." Mam came into the kitchen from the hall, where she'd been talking to Kathy Henderson on the phone, checking on Chad. "I gave Bonnie one of my sleeping pills."

"I hope they work better for her than they do for you," Olivia said.

"Oh, they work," Mam said. "When I take a pill, I can sleep up to six hours, instead of my usual four. Want an oatmeal cookie?"

Olivia just shook her head as she watched my cousin straighten the snacks and wipe away crumbs on the butcher-block counter.

I took a deep breath. "The news isn't good, is it?"

Olivia grimaced. "No, but they'll stay out there awhile yet. Could be he'll come in with the tide, or maybe he'll float up out near the sand bar in a few days. Could be we never will find him." She looked at Mam. "Any chance Bonnie's husband can get some leave time and come home? I expect she could use his support about now."

Mam said, "I do know she's e-mailed Tom, but she said the navy doesn't send guys home unless a family member is in the hospital or dies. Almost drowned doesn't count. His ship is somewhere in the Persian Gulf, so hopefully he can get a call through or e-mail her."

As if on cue, the wall phone started ringing.

"That may be Tom." Mam hurried to get it. "Hello . . . All right . . . Nine o'clock, yes, ma'am . . . Yes, ma'am . . . She's sleeping. . . . Yes, ma'am. Okay, bye." She hung up. "That was Miss Augusta. She was adamant. She wants Bonnie to come see her at Pinckney at nine o'clock tomorrow morning."

Olivia looked at her watch and rose to go. "I have to get back and report in. Will—Major McLeod, I mean—says he'll call you later."

"Thanks," I said, walking her to the door.

It was still hot outside, but a breeze was coming off the water as the tide came in. This seemed like the longest day ever, and it wouldn't be dark for hours. Night comes so late in the summertime. Leaning against the porch rail, I watched Olivia's patrol car drive slowly down the beach road. Two carloads of teens cruised by, whistling loudly out their passenger windows at the cute girl lounging on the deck across the street. I felt so old. I turned to go in. Through the screen door, I saw Mam circling the coffee table like she was playing her own private version of musical chairs. What was she up to now?

Then I saw Bonnie's open laptop on the coffee table.

"You are not, I repeat, not, going to snoop in her e-mails," I said.

"I just want to see if Tom has messaged back yet," she said innocently.

"Absolutely not."

"Okay, I'll wait, even though Bonnie wouldn't care if I read her mail."

"You don't know that. She didn't give you her password, did she?"

"Well, no." Mam hesitated. "But I think it's—"

"Stop! I don't want to know. Mam, I think it's time for you to go home. J. T. and Cissy will be wanting dinner. I'm going to walk down to Mama's and bring Doc back with me. If Bonnie wants me to, I'll sleep here tonight."

"What are you going to eat for supper?" Mam went back in the kitchen. "I better stay and fix y'all something."

"Mam! Just because I don't cook doesn't mean I don't know how." Really. She gets more like our mamas every day. "If anyone is hungry, I'm perfectly capable of making sandwiches or fixing something."

"Or ordering pizza!"

"That's an option, too." I looked out the kitchen window. "Uh-oh. Don't leave yet. There's a TV truck pulling into the driveway."

Mam leaned over my shoulder so she could see. "Really! I'll just go out there and tell them to leave! They are trying to exploit a tragedy."

"I'll go," I said. Mam can be a loose cannon. "If I make a brief statement on behalf of the family, like what I told R. W. over the phone, they'll go away satisfied. Otherwise, they'll find some goober on the street who doesn't know squat but wants to be on TV."

"Well, at least fix your hair and put on some lipstick," Mam insisted. "You look like something the cat dragged in."

Tact is not among Mam's virtues. But sometimes it's easier to comply than argue. "It's not a fashion shoot," I said, even as I took the brush from her.

A few minutes later, she was shoving me out the screen door. "You'll do," she said.

I recognized the clean-cut young reporter from one of the Charleston stations. He had signaled the video guy to start taping as soon as I stepped onto the porch, and now he was eagerly holding a microphone.

"Mrs. Tyler," he said, "can you please tell our viewers what you're feeling?"

This was why I had quit being a TV reporter umpteen years ago.

"I'm not Mrs. Tyler," I said firmly. "I'm her cousin. Mrs. Tyler is with her sons, and she asks that you please respect their privacy. Our family is very grateful to Dr. Jenkins for his heroic actions, and our prayers are with him and his family. We also wish to thank all who have been of help during this difficult time."

As soon as I stopped, the reporter started with more obnoxious questions. He was obviously angling for a network pickup. "Does young Ben know how to swim? Where was Mrs. Tyler when he almost drowned? What is her relationship with Dr. Jenkins? Did she know he had a heart condition?"

Geez, Louise. "Dr. Jenkins is a longtime friend of our family and a community leader. He is also a man of courage and . . ." My voice started to break. I shook my head. I couldn't go on.

The reporter was still shouting questions as I shut the door.

🧠

The phone rang continuously. At first, I answered it, hoping it was Tom. Finally, though, after fending off well-meaning neighbors, reassuring our parents, and talking to Mam four or five times, I turned down the ring and started screening calls through the answering machine. Aunt Boodie and Uncle James don't have caller ID, and neither do my parents. The mamas want to talk to everybody.

"Screening's not polite," Mam reprimanded me.

"You're lucky I took your call," I retorted.

"I called to see if Tom has called," she said. "Is Bonnie awake?"

"Not now. It's after eleven. And no, Tom hasn't called."

"You could check her e-mail."

"No, not going there. Besides, Bonnie checked when she was up, before and after supper."

Mam was diverted. "What did you feed them?"

"Grilled cheese sandwiches," I said. "And no, I didn't burn them."

"Did you ask Bonnie if she knows that R. stands for Wayne?"

"No! We agreed to wait. Leave her be. We'll talk tomorrow before she goes to see Miss Augusta."

"I wonder what's with that command performance. Do you—"

"Gotta go," I interrupted. "Another call."

"Mama doesn't have call waiting."

"My cell." I hung up on her and picked up my phone. It's a mystery to me how I can get a signal in this house and not at Mama's right down the street, unless I'm hanging out a second-story window. "Hey, Will."

"Sorry it's so late, but I wanted to see if you're okay." His voice was soft.

"I'm okay," I said, then contradicted myself. "No, I'm not. I'm an emotional wreck. Can you come over?"

"Five minutes." He hung up.

I slipped out the screen door, moving away from the light, where moths were flitting in circles. As soon as Will opened the door of his truck, I was running down the stairs. I ran straight to him and threw my arms around his neck, my face pressed against his solid, reassuring chest, hanging on for dear life. Today had scared me silly, but I knew one thing. I loved Will. And I wasn't going to let R. stand for regret.

CHAPTER NINETEEN
Lucky Charm

"Are you asleep, Aunt Lindsey?"

"No, Ben, just resting my eyes." Heavens, I sounded like Miss Augusta. I had been awake on and off for hours, my mind trying to untangle the events and emotions of the last few days. "Are Sam and your mother up?"

"Sam's with Mama talking to Daddy on the phone." Ben, wearing plaid boxers and seemingly none the worse for wear after yesterday, climbed on the sofa beside me. "I already talked to him. He's on his ship. Can I watch TV?"

"How about you go get dressed while I fix you some breakfast?"

"Do you know how to make blueberry pancakes?"

Oh, great. Another relative who assumed I was cooking impaired.

"I do, but we don't have time today because we're all going to Pinckney very soon." I knew Bonnie wouldn't let the boys out of her sight today.

Ben's grin lit up the room. "Cool! We can help Posey with the sprinklers!"

"If he says so. You can also throw Doc his tennis ball." I looked at my dog, who was sacked out on the floor after our sunrise walk on the beach. He had raised his ears upon hearing his name, and now the word *ball* had him thumping his tail. "Want some cereal?" Both boy and dog stood up. "I saw Lucky Charms in the pantry."

❧

Bonnie stood up from the chair in my office. "I guess it's time to go see what Miss Augusta wants." She held out her hand. "But she should be happy. I brought her this."

"The diamond charm!" Mam reached for the glittery silver. "Where did you find it?"

"I didn't," Bonnie said. "Wayne did." She took a deep breath and tried to smile. "He gave it to me at the Point yesterday before . . . before everything. He found it after the fireworks, he said. Don't tell Miss Augusta, please. I'd just as soon she not know."

Mam and I nodded. Bonnie didn't want Miss Augusta to know how close she and Wayne had been.

"We need to talk about Wayne," Mam ventured. "There's something—"

"Not now," Bonnie said. "Let me get through this first. I don't want to keep Miss Augusta waiting."

Mam waited until she thought Bonnie was out of earshot, then gave one of her whispers that can ruffle the pages of a hymnal in church. "I wouldn't want to be in Bonnie's shoes right now. I think Miss Augusta wants a come-to-Jesus meeting between military wives. She's going to remind her to behave herself."

"I guess," I said. "Bonnie's holding herself together pretty well. She was crying when she got off the phone with Tom, but she told the boys she was just so happy that their daddy had called."

"I believe that," Mam said. "I cried that time in the hospital, I was so glad to see J. T."

And I had cried last night with Will, but I didn't tell Mam. We were a weepy bunch, all right. "Here," I said, handing Mam a calendar. "Help me figure out the August guide schedule while we're waiting on Bonnie."

Actually, we didn't have to wait long before Bonnie reappeared in the doorway. She looked a little pale, but her eyes were dry.

"That was quick," Mam said. "What did she say?"

Bonnie waved her hand. "This and that. Y'know, stiff upper lip in times of crisis, etcetera, etcetera. But she got really excited about the charm. She's calling Ross Savage now." She sighed. "I know it's supposed to be this precious gem, but it still looks like a geegaw to me. And I have to say, I couldn't give a rip about jewels right now. There are more important things in this world. Where are my boys?"

"Ben and Sam are in the side yard with Posey and Doc," I said. "Marietta's making them cookies. She made you a coconut cake."

"Ooh, coconut!" Bonnie savored the word. She looked at her watch. Somewhere in the world, it was time for coconut cake. "Quick, though, before the plantation opens, Miss Augusta wants us to get a box for her out of the attic. She doesn't remember exactly where it is, but it's about this big"—she gestured with her hands—"and it has a Canadian shipping label on it."

"Canadian?" Mam repeated. "Then it came from Canada."

"Obviously," said Bonnie. "It's some of Julia's things that were sent to Miss Augusta after the accident. She looked through them at the time, she said, but then she packed them up again and hasn't had the heart to go through them since. Now, she wants me to have Julia's charm bracelet because I had to give my teapot charm back. Like I said, I could care less." She stopped. "About Wayne . . ."

Mam saw an opening. "Wayne's not the man you thought, Bonnie. He had some secrets."

"I know," Bonnie said. "R. is for Richie, he told me."

"When?" Mam and I asked simultaneously.

"Yesterday, when he gave me back the charm. Some guy he knew since forever yelled, 'Hey, Richie!' at him from the beach, and I asked him about it. Then I had another epiphany, I guess. I said, 'You were Becky's boyfriend in high school.'"

"What did he say?" Mam asked breathlessly. "Why didn't you tell us before now that you knew? Was he in the graveyard?"

"I think so," Bonnie said wearily. "We had only started talking about it when I heard Sam yell." Her eyes started to well. "I'm a terrible mother. If I hadn't been so intent with Wayne, I'd have seen Ben and Chad with the float. Oh, I feel so guilty! It's all my fault!" She was crying in earnest now.

Mam would have none of it. "No, it is not your fault!" She pushed a Kleenex at Bonnie. "Don't you ever think that!"

"But if Wayne hadn't—"

"Wayne chose to rescue the boys," I said gently. If she didn't stop crying, we'd all be weepy.

Mam realized it, too. "Stop blubbering, Bonnie! We all feel awful, but crying isn't going to help. Now, what did Wayne tell you about Becky?"

Bonnie hiccupped. "Something about Becky having the wrong idea, and it wasn't supposed to happen that way, and that he still felt guilty." She hiccupped again, then said, "I can understand that."

"Did he kill her?" Mam brought Bonnie back on point. "Or was it Fort? Did you ask him how she died? Maybe an accident?"

"I don't know, I don't know!" Bonnie was shredding the Kleenex. "I think it might have been suicide. The last thing he said before we heard Sam was, 'Becky killed Becky.'" She looked at us hopefully. "Do you think it could have happened that way, that Becky killed herself?"

Suicide. We hadn't thought of that.

"She was really unhappy," I said.

"And she had a secret plan." Mam frowned. "Poor Becky! We'll have to think on this." She looked at her sister. "C'mon, now, pull yourself together. We need to go get that box for Miss Augusta before the tourists arrive. You don't want to let her see you've been crying. Go wash your face and redo your makeup. You look like—"

"—something the cat dragged in!" Bonnie and I finished the sentence for her.

"That, too." Mam had the grace to grin. "Actually, I was going to say you look like the dog's dinner."

"Eww!" Bonnie made a face. "Thanks a lot, sis."

I picked up the plantation keys off my desk. "No point in redoing your makeup yet. It's hot as blazes in the attic. We'll all be Purina if we don't get in and out of there quickly."

"Fine with me," Mam said. "You know how I get claustrophobia."

"We know!" Bonnie said. "Everybody knows!"

❧

The attic wasn't quite as hot as I expected. Set at slow-bake this early, it would be on broil by noon. An ancient revolving floor fan spread more dust than air. I looked around for spiders. "I'll take this area, and you two start over there." I pointed to the darkest of corners under the eaves, where several boxes were stacked. Spider heaven.

"Oh, look at this old red guide dress. It would have been perfect for the parade," Mam said.

"Let it go," I said.

"Maybe next year," Bonnie added from the far corner.

"Cissy would have looked darling in it." Mam sighed, then sneezed. "You know, I am still flabbergasted Miss Augusta's letting us look through Julia's things."

"Look *for* Julia's things," Bonnie said. "I don't think we're supposed to go through them."

"Well, how are we going to find the charm bracelet?" Mam asked.

"I think she wants us to bring her the box," Bonnie said.

I shifted some plastic bins holding Christmas decorations and felt myself starting to sweat. "First, we have to find it."

"Hey!" Bonnie called from the shadows. "I think this is it." She emerged from under the eaves and plunked down a dusty brown box on a broken wicker chair.

"So, do we open it or not?" Mam had her trusty floral knife in hand.

"Open it," Bonnie said. "The packing tape's cracking from age anyway. I think we can tear it." She gave a little tug at one corner. "Hand me your knife, Mam."

I think we were all holding our breath just a little bit. It was like a lost treasure box. Julia was such a mystery to the three of us. Now, we were ready to add some more pieces to the puzzle.

Bonnie pulled the flaps back and lifted out a moldy leather purse. I set it to one side as Mam reached for more items. A troll doll with shocking pink hair. A yellowing paperback copy of *Gone With the Wind* and another of Tolkien's *Return of the King*. A French-English dictionary. Julia had eclectic reading tastes. I picked up a small cedar box with a Charleston, S.C., decal on the front with palm trees. "Bonnie, this may be a jewelry box." I handed it over to her.

She raised the lid. "You're right. And here's the charm bracelet with all the states on it that Julia visited, just like Miss Augusta described."

Mam took it from her. "These are real silver. Look how tarnished they are. Here's a tennis racket, and a little merry-go-round. And a teapot like yours, Bonnie, only . . ."

"Was there supposed to be another teapot?" I asked.

Bonnie took the bracelet and peered at the charm. "Now, *this* looks like a real diamond. See how it sparkles, even though it's dirty?" She rubbed it on her cutoff blue jeans, the other charms jangling together, and then held it up to a slant of sunlight. The charm twinkled among the dust motes. "But how did Queen Charlotte's diamond end up on Julia's bracelet?"

"Maybe Becky gave it to her," I said. "Miss Eliza could have given it to her—to Becky, I mean."

"Hmm." Mam rocked back on her heels. "Another mystery. We'll have to ask Miss Augusta." She pulled a spiral-bound notebook from the box. "This is funny."

Bonnie and I both knew she meant funny peculiar, not funny ha-ha.

"It's like the one I found that belonged to Becky." She flipped open the pages. "Even the writing's the same. Julia was Becky's teacher. I suppose she could have held onto this as some sort of keepsake."

"Let me see." Bonnie took the notebook and went to the small-paned window, where the light was better. "The writing does look like Becky's." She was quiet for a moment as she scanned the first page. "Oh, wow!"

"What? What?" Mam yipped.

"Listen to this and tell me what you think. It's dated August 9, 1971." Bonnie started reading: " 'Last night, I dreamed about Indigo again. Somehow, my subconscious must have realized it was the third anniversary, our birthday. We were in the cemetery laughing, and then I was crying. It was that quick. I still don't understand how a life can end so sudden. If that tree limb hadn't been cracked, if that headstone hadn't been right under the tree . . . I have never been able to write about that night. This is my first diary entry in three years. I remember how hot it was, and the way the moon looked through the trees. Maybe if I write about it, I won't have nightmares anymore. Maybe the real J. will be exorcised and I won't feel guilty or haunted.' "

Bonnie stopped. I heard Mam's indrawn breath. The fan stirred the warm air. I looked at my cousins.

"Wayne said Becky killed Becky." Bonnie's voice trembled.

"No, Becky killed Julia," Mam said.

"You're both right," I said. "Becky killed Julia so she could become Julia."

No one said anything for a moment as we let the import of our discovery sink in.

"We found Julia," Mam said in a wondering voice. "She never left the island." She looked at the notebook in Bonnie's hand. "Do you think Becky really killed her? Maybe it was an accident."

"Maybe," Bonnie said sternly. "But she sure as shooting assumed Julia's identity." She turned to another page. "Right here, she says she has liked being Julia, even though she calls herself Julie or"—Bonnie put on a French accent—"Ju-*lee*."

"It's close to *jolie*, French for 'pretty,' " I said. "Becky always wanted to be pretty like Julia."

"She wanted to *be* Julia." Bonnie was scanning more entries. "I'm beginning not to like Becky very much. She'd have called herself Whistlin' Dixie if that got her what she wanted. The proof is all in here. We need to read this all the way through."

"What are we going to tell Miss Augusta?" Mam looked stricken. "We have to tell her, don't we? Lord, I hope she doesn't have a spell, or worse. Remember, she had that stroke or 'brain event' just six months ago."

"And I'm going to have heatstroke if we stay up here," I said. "Bring the box and let's go downstairs to the second floor. We'll read it and figure out how to tell Miss Augusta. We do have to tell her."

Bonnie nodded. "This secret doesn't belong to us."

November 7

Sometimes, it is hard to live a secret life. You never can really talk about when you were a kid or in high school, because it is so easy to make a mistake. Julia would be 25 now. I will always remember the look on her face right before she fell. It was stupid climbing the tree, but it was our farewell to Indigo. Richie was standing on the bench, and we had been sitting on the low limb swinging our legs. I was next to the trunk so I stood up first, and Julia was hanging onto me for balance. Right before she fell, she gave a little gasp and had this strange, surprised look. Then my foot was tangled with hers and I grabbed the trunk and she was gone. I think I screamed, but she didn't make a sound. Richie was kneeling by her by the time I got down, and he said her neck was broken, that I had killed her. He was crying. I knew then he didn't love me. He loved her. Now, I am her, but I will never see him again.

CHAPTER TWENTY
Coming Home

It rained the morning Julia came home. By then, we were well into August and hurricane season. A tropical storm brushed by, ending the drought, cleansing the air, and washing away the lingering smell of smoke.

This sunrise had brought a few showers, but by the time we gathered on the bluff at Pinckney, the gray clouds were parting on a cooling breeze. Miss Augusta moved away from the shelter of the big black umbrella Bonnie was holding and opened the iron gate to her family plot. She looked small and frail but also proud and determined.

When we had first told her the news on that sultry July day, she had looked puzzled and disbelieving even as she took the notebook and charm bracelet.

"I . . . I don't understand," she said, letting the evidence fall into her lap. "How can this be true? My Julia?" Tears glazed her hooded eyes. "Marietta! Where is Marietta? Does she know?"

Marietta, standing in the doorway, immediately came to Miss Augusta. "I knows," she said, sitting on an ottoman and reaching out both hands to hold Miss Augusta's. "This a hard thing, but the good Lord will see it right."

Miss Augusta clasped Marietta's hands and appeared to go into a sort of trance. She was with us but not with us. As she spoke in a low monotone, we listened, spellbound.

"Oh, Julia, my heart is breaking again. It breaks for you and all of us who loved you. Here all along . . . all along . . . I cannot forgive them for what they did. Such terrible lies . . . I understand why Rebecca—Becky—left. I didn't really know her, but I should have seen her unhappiness and desperation. Eliza should have done something. I think she knew but refused to believe it. Like his drinking, she looked the other way. This was so much worse. It would be hard to believe, your own son . . . No one talked of such things. So many secrets . . . And Wayne knowing all these years, and still he said he loved you. Oh, Julia, you never left me, never left the island."

Miss Augusta suddenly gripped Marietta's hands even harder, as if she could channel the other woman's strength and ease the burden of her own sorrow. She blinked rapidly several times. The distant look disappeared. She was with us again.

"Of course, Julia would have left," she said in a more normal, if shaky, voice. "She'd written that letter explaining why, the one Becky found and sent. Her father was so angry. He thought she had betrayed her country, betrayed him. He wouldn't talk about her. She had her own money, of course, from my father. It came to her when she was twenty-one, to do with what she liked. I hoped she wouldn't fritter it away on one of her causes." Miss Augusta sniffed and cleared her throat. "But I never doubted she had gone to Canada. She and her father had such bitter arguments about the war." She looked at us as if begging for understanding. "I took his side. He was my husband. You see, I always thought she'd come back."

Marietta clucked softly in agreement. "She would have. We knows that now." She ducked her head toward the dusty box Mam had set next to Miss Augusta's chair. "I remember the day that box come. You shut yourself in here for a long time. Then you gave it to me and said put it in the attic. It been there ever since."

"I couldn't bear going through her things," Miss Augusta said. "I found some books and the jewelry box. I thought maybe the little gold locket I gave her would be in there, and her pearls, but there was just the bracelet and some cheap earrings. I cried then, and I couldn't stop." Her voice quavered. "I remembered that it was the locket that helped identify her. It had her initials on it. What remained of it was in an envelope that came with her ashes. We buried it with her." She closed her eyes.

"Becky sold the pearls," Bonnie said, her own lashes wet. "It's in the notebook. She was running out of money. The locket would have been next, then the Mustang, and then the diamond charm."

I continued, "She left her father's dog tags and her high-school ring with Julia, but she took the charm to bring her luck."

Mam, who had remained unusually quiet, piped up. "She stole that, too. Maybe it's part of the curse of the Comforts, Lindsey."

"The curse of the Comforts!" Miss Augusta sat upright, dropping Marietta's hands. "I've never heard such foolishness. Marietta, what nonsense have you been telling them?"

Marietta shook her head and stood up creakily. "I going to get you some tea. You want anything else?"

"No, thank you." She looked at all of us. "It's a good thing I called Mr. Savage earlier about Bonnie's charm." Her smile was mirthless. "Of course, it's not the right charm, but he's on his way. I think we're going to need his help bringing Julia home to Pinckney."

❀

Now, the courtly lawyer, who had been standing next to the tall Pinckney family tombstone, came forward to meet Miss Augusta. He escorted her to the plot Posey had dug at dawn in the soft green earth, where the simple coffin already rested.

Miss Augusta was right. It had helped that Ross Savage was

both her lawyer and Miss Eliza's, and had friends in very high places. I didn't know all the ins and outs. As Bonnie said, it was probably better not to know. As an officer of the court, she didn't want to be obliged to reveal any knowledge of possible illegal activities. As a reporter, I wouldn't have to reveal my sources if I didn't have any, and Will and I had agreed not to discuss it. As for Mam, the fewer details she knew, the better. Of course, she wanted to know them all and kept busy speculating.

"You know, the diamond has something to do with it," she told us one day. "I bet they're using it to pay off Fort so he'll release Becky's bones—which are really Julia's—to Miss Augusta. There has to be some reason he's accepting a plea bargain."

"Maybe it's because he's guilty," Bonnie said dryly. But she also thought weight had been brought to bear on the last of the Baileys so he wouldn't go blabbing. Even though Becky was dead, Fort wouldn't want to risk being branded a sexual predator, in or out of prison. "Technically, of course, the diamond doesn't belong to Miss Augusta. It never left the Bailey family. But Fort still thinks Lindsey's the one who bought it in the box of jewelry at the estate sale. And she probably has the bill of sale stuffed somewhere because she never throws anything away."

I smirked. I was pretty sure the sales slip was in my glove compartment, or else in the box that had held my blue plate. Wherever, whatever. I wasn't interested in the kind of charmed life that diamond appeared to bestow. I like happy endings. Meanwhile, I was on Google alert for news of a museum or collector somewhere acquiring a priceless piece of jewelry having once belonged to Queen Charlotte. It would be identified as having come from "a private family collection," to protect Fort's privacy. Heck, perhaps the royal family wanted it back, in which case we might never know.

Miss Augusta had the last notebook. She didn't know I had a copy. Every now and then, I would take it out and read it again. I really didn't know what to think of Becky. Yes, she had been selfish. But she also had been in pain, afraid of Fort and stunned by Richie's—Wayne's—last-minute betrayal. He had been in love with Julia, not her. Once Julia was dead, he didn't want to leave. Becky had turned on him, forcing him to help in her conspiracy. Otherwise, she would tell everyone he had killed Julia and raped her.

Becky was cunning, no doubt about that, and lucky in some ways. Lucky that Wayne's father was a dentist, so he could switch the dental records just in case, and that she and Julia were of similar size and coloring. Forensics weren't so cutting edge back then. DNA was still in the future, like all the things we took for granted that had changed our lives, from the fall of the Berlin Wall and the events of 9/11 to the Internet and iPods. Almost forty years of history. Most of my lifetime.

I wondered if I could have done what Becky did. Not killing Julia, either intentionally or by accident. But having the sheer nerve to seize the moment. It had taken bravery—or at least bravura—for Becky to reinvent herself as Julia, to run away and live in Quebec, where people didn't understand her high-school French and funny accent. She was closer to Queen Charlotte than she realized, another teenage stranger in a strange land. Or maybe it was just willful ignorance, the impetuosity of youth that saw only roses and no thorns.

Mam was carrying a wreath of red roses and magnolia leaves she'd stayed up all night making. Marietta, wearing a black Sunday-go-to-meeting dress and a small, feathered hat, had her Bible in one gloved hand. She dabbed at her eyes with an embroidered hanky in the other. "See?" She had showed it to us earlier. "I teach Julia how to do this when she just a bitty thing, and then she made me this one for my birthday."

Bonnie and I both had perfect red roses. We passed them to Miss Augusta, who paused before letting them fall on Julia's coffin. I wondered what Bonnie was thinking. Wayne's body had not yet been found. He was another enigma, a weak and confused young man who became a stand-up guy. How had he lived with his guilt?

Miss Augusta had decided that Julia would not lie next to Becky's ashes. Accordingly, Posey had removed the urn, and Mr. Savage had it reinterred at Indigo Hill in the Bailey family plot, next to Becky's memory stone. As far as anyone knew, these were the cremated remains of the bones found by the back fence. Some secrets are best left buried—or reburied.

For an old woman, Marietta had a surprisingly strong and true voice: "Swing low, sweet chariot, coming for to carry me home . . ."

❦

The next day, Mam and I drove Bonnie to the airport in Charleston to catch the first of the flights that would take her to Spain. Tom would be there waiting for her so they could be together for his short leave. The boys were staying on Indigo now that our parents were home for a while. The mamas were irked they'd missed the sweet corn but were gorging on peaches and tomatoes.

I glanced in the rearview mirror at the sound of a siren.

Mam shouted in my ear, "Lindsey, blue light!"

"I see it, and I'm not deaf!" I eased off the gas and signaled to pull off on the shoulder.

"Oops. How fast were you going?" asked Bonnie.

"Well, I don't know," I said. "I wasn't actually paying attention." I had been distracted all morning.

"Hey, isn't that the same young guy who stopped us the last time?" Mam laughed as I reached in my purse for my wallet. "Lindsey, wait a darn minute! I just noticed—"

"Shh, he's coming." I opened my window and adjusted the A.C. so it would hit me directly.

"But Lindsey . . . Bonnie, did you see?" Mam turned in the passenger seat, tangling her seat belt.

"Hello, Ms. Fox. License and registration, please."

"Hello, Officer Walters." I handed him my open wallet.

"Very good," he said. "I wanted to see if you had a South Carolina driver's license to go with your new plate. The address says 2500 Pinckney Plantation Road. Are you living on the plantation?"

He made it sound like Tara before the war. The reality was Miss Augusta's old suite on the big house's second floor, which she had abandoned when she could no longer manage the narrow stairs. She had urged me to move in, saying I'd have more space and privacy than at my folks'. And I could bring my pets. "That dog follows you everywhere anyway," she said. "And he has a good loud bark." Peaches the cat had the run of the second floor but spent most days curled on the window seat in my bedroom. Mama was sorry to see me go, but not the animals. Too much fur for her sinuses.

"I'm at Pinckney for the time being," I told Officer Walters. "Did you stop me just to see if I'd changed my license?"

He blushed. "Uh, yes, ma'am, it's my job. And since the major's back, I thought maybe you might be staying. . . ." His voice trailed off uncertainly.

Mam couldn't stand it any longer. "Of course she is! They're engaged!" She grabbed my hand for Bonnie to see.

"Oh, for land's sake!" said Bonnie. "Look at that ring! How beautiful! Oh sorry, officer, didn't mean to interrupt you."

"Sure we did. This is *big* news!" squealed Mam.

"Well, congratulations," the young deputy said sheepishly with a hint of a smile. "I'll be on my way now. Drive safely, ladies."

"Officer Walters, could you keep this, uh, big news a secret, for today at least?" I asked. "I haven't told my mama yet—or anyone, in fact." I looked at my cousins. I'd been waiting all morning for them to notice the ring.

"Your secret is safe with me," he said, backing off. "Have a good day."

Mam was about to pull my arm out my socket. "Okay, let us look at that rock!"

I wiggled my finger so the diamond sparkled even more.

"A gorgeous setting," Bonnie said. "Was it in his family?"

"No," I said. "It's new, just for me." This ring really was all mine. "We might use Nanny's wedding band, though."

"She'd like that," Bonnie said approvingly.

"I'm just so excited we get to plan another wedding!" Mam was going into overdrive. "When is it? Have you thought about flowers yet? You'll have it at Pinckney, of course."

"Whoa, slow down," I said, putting the car in gear. "Will and I haven't gotten that far yet." I pulled out and headed for the drawbridge. It was open to traffic. Officer Walters was right—we were having a good day.

Mam and Bonnie kept talking on top of one another.

"I think fall."

"Shrimp and grits for the reception."

"Beach music."

"Hair up or down?"

"Blue-and-white, maybe?"

"Listen up, cousins!" I raised my voice. "I know some things. No way am I wearing a hoop skirt. And absolutely no Pinckney purple!"

Epilogue

On the hottest night of the year, he hid among the thick bushes and trailing vines at the edge of the graveyard. He could see the three of them in the moonlight falling on the marble tomb, but he was shrouded in darkness.

The girls sat on the oak limb, and the boy was standing on a stone bench. They were talking, laughing. The girls stood up, clinging to one another.

His hand found a rock in the dirt. He threw it at the tree. Now, they would have to notice him.

He saw the girl fall. A scream ripped through the night. He could smell his own fear. He ran. This was one secret Rabbit would take to his grave.

Acknowledgments

Way Down Dead in Dixie is a work of fiction. You won't find Pinckney Plantation, Indigo Island, or Granville County on any map of the South Carolina Low Country. Like the characters in the book, they are products of our imagination. Where actual place names or historical figures occur in the narrative, they are used fictitiously.

Many family members and friends helped us in the writing of "the third book." We would especially like to thank our parents, Frances Pate and Boodie and Robert Godwin; first readers Rebecca Swain Vadnie, Kathy Roe, and Aly Greer; the Edisto Island Historical Society; Barbara Neiderhiser and Cinderella; Bonnie King and King's Market of Edisto Island; the Edisto Book Club; the Third Friday Book Club (Orlando); Katy Moore; Nancy Lassiter; Patti Morrison; Ed Malles; Nancy's friends at the *Orlando Sentinel*; Jackie and Suzy Sanderson; our "mystery mom," Kathy Hogan Trocheck; and the entire staff of John F. Blair, Publisher. Thanks, too, to the many readers, booksellers, and librarians who helped make our previous novels, *Fiddle Dee Death* and *Marsh Madness*, so successful and who welcomed "the Cousins" when we were on tour. Again, you are our people.

Caroline Cousins is a pseudonym for Nancy Pate and her "one-and-a-half-times" first cousins, sisters Meg Herndon and Gail Greer. (Their mothers are sisters, and their fathers are first cousins.) Meg, who owns a specialty floral business, lives on Edisto Island, South Carolina, as does Gail, a former plantation tour guide. Nancy, former longtime book critic for the *Orlando Sentinel*, divides her time between Edisto and Orlando, Florida.